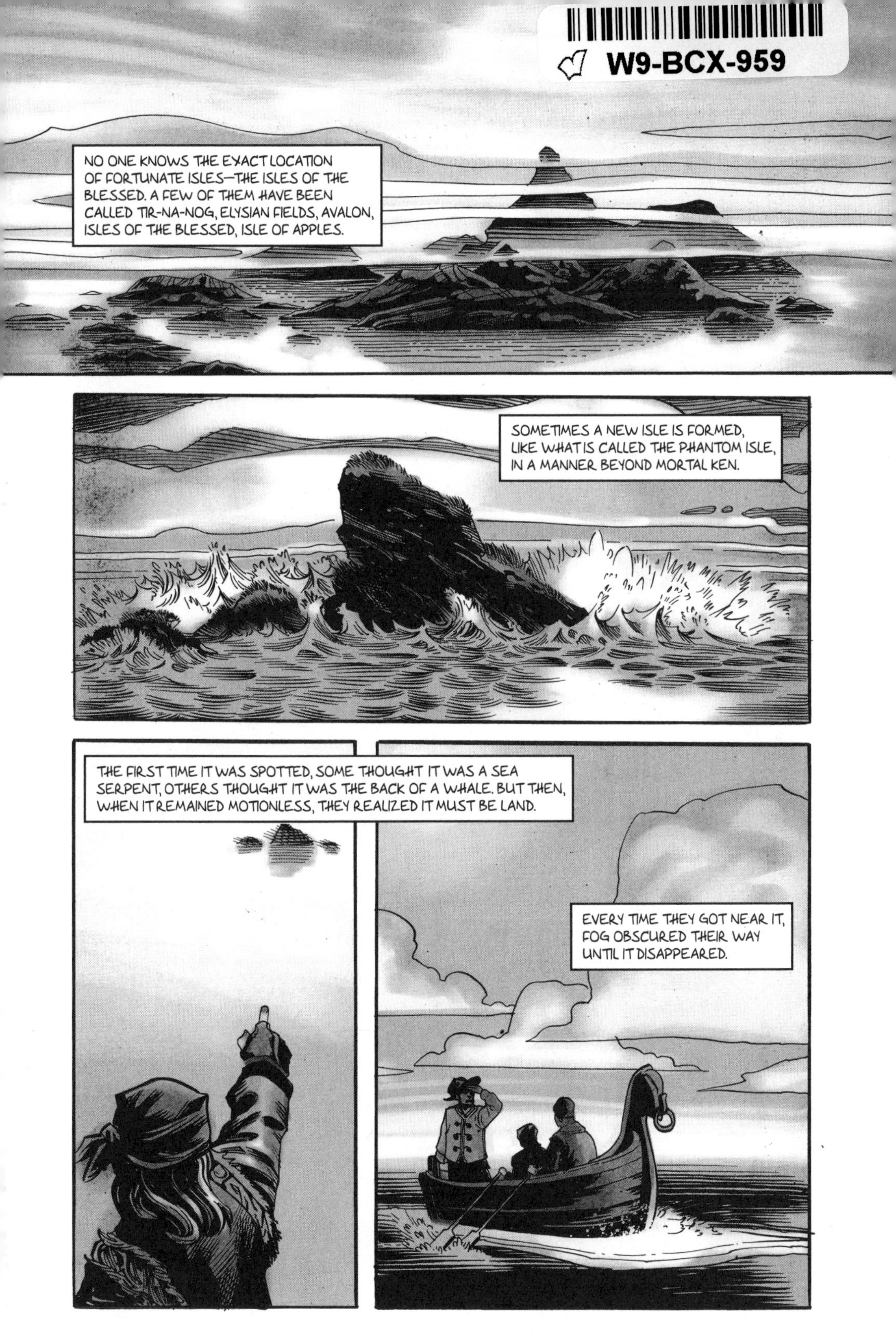
NO ONE KNOWS THE EXACT LOCATION OF FORTUNATE ISLES—THE ISLES OF THE BLESSED. A FEW OF THEM HAVE BEEN CALLED TIR-NA-NOG, ELYSIAN FIELDS, AVALON, ISLES OF THE BLESSED, ISLE OF APPLES.
SOMETIMES A NEW ISLE IS FORMED, LIKE WHAT IS CALLED THE PHANTOM ISLE, IN A MANNER BEYOND MORTAL KEN.
THE FIRST TIME IT WAS SPOTTED, SOME THOUGHT IT WAS A SEA SERPENT, OTHERS THOUGHT IT WAS THE BACK OF A WHALE. BUT THEN, WHEN IT REMAINED MOTIONLESS, THEY REALIZED IT MUST BE LAND.
EVERY TIME THEY GOT NEAR IT, FOG OBSCURED THEIR WAY UNTIL IT DISAPPEARED.

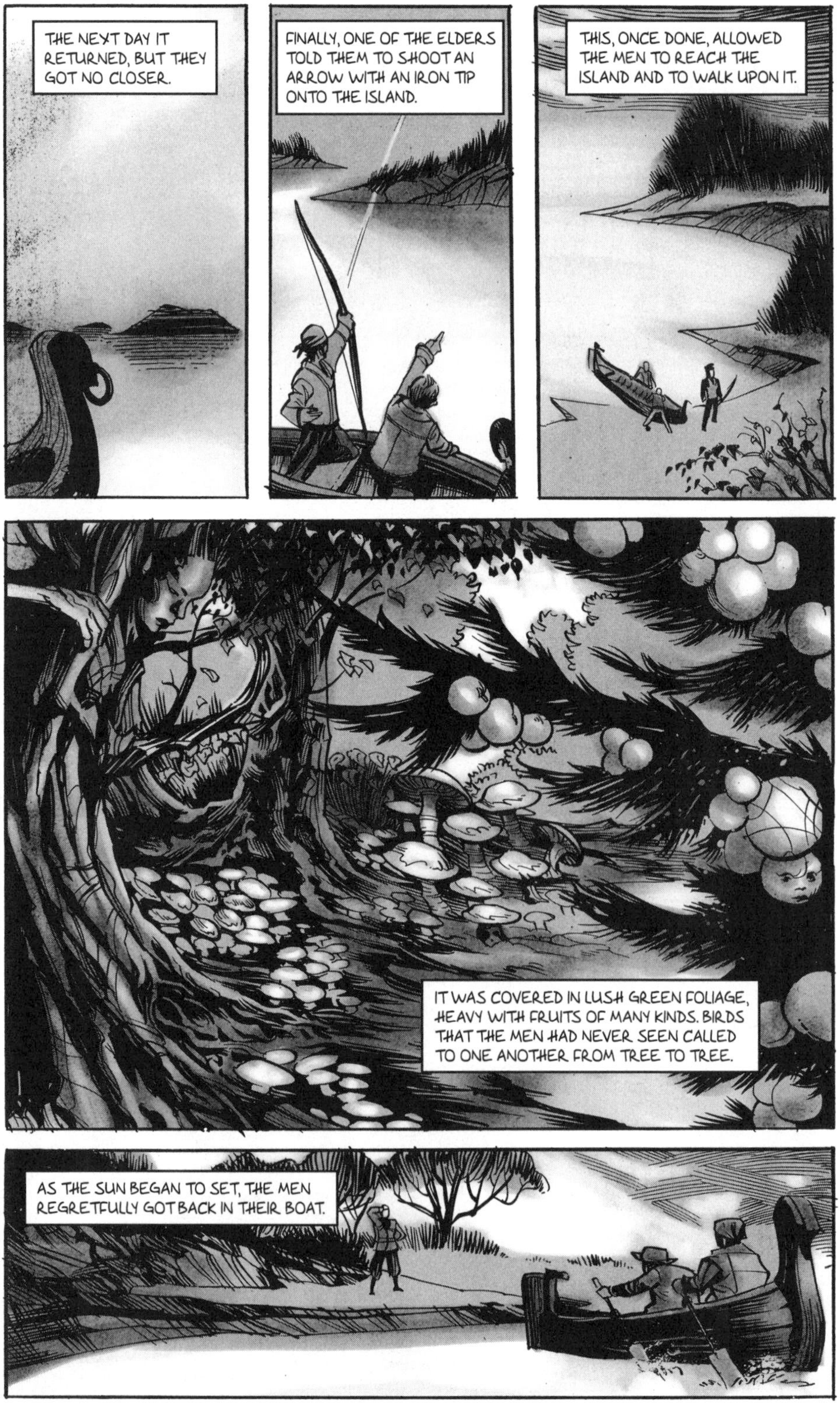
THE NEXT DAY IT RETURNED, BUT THEY GOT NO CLOSER.
FINALLY, ONE OF THE ELDERS TOLD THEM TO SHOOT AN ARROW WITH AN IRON TIP ONTO THE ISLAND.
THIS, ONCE DONE, ALLOWED THE MEN TO REACH THE ISLAND AND TO WALK UPON IT.
IT WAS COVERED IN LUSH GREEN FOLIAGE, HEAVY WITH FRUITS OF MANY KINDS. BIRDS THAT THE MEN HAD NEVER SEEN CALLED TO ONE ANOTHER FROM TREE TO TREE.
AS THE SUN BEGAN TO SET, THE MEN REGRETFULLY GOT BACK IN THEIR BOAT.

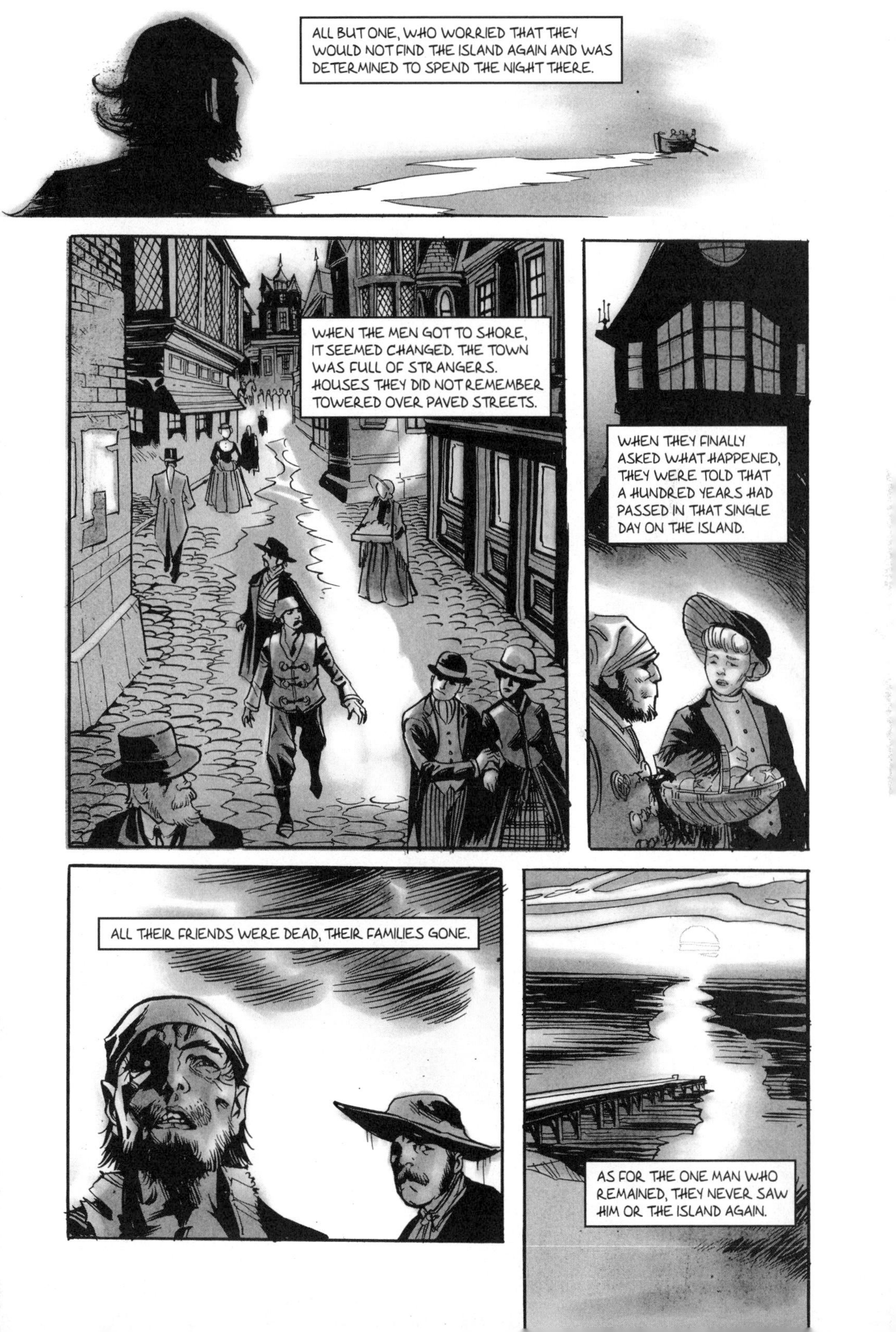
ALL BUT ONE, WHO WORRIED THAT THEY WOULD NOT FIND THE ISLAND AGAIN AND WAS DETERMINED TO SPEND THE NIGHT THERE.
WHEN THE MEN GOT TO SHORE, IT SEEMED CHANGED. THE TOWN WAS FULL OF STRANGERS. HOUSES THEY DID NOT REMEMBER TOWERED OVER PAVED STREETS.
WHEN THEY FINALLY ASKED WHAT HAPPENED, THEY WERE TOLD THAT A HUNDRED YEARS HAD PASSED IN THAT SINGLE DAY ON THE ISLAND.
ALL THEIR FRIENDS WERE DEAD, THEIR FAMILIES GONE.
AS FOR THE ONE MAN WHO REMAINED, THEY NEVER SAW HIM OR THE ISLAND AGAIN.

The Good Neighbors

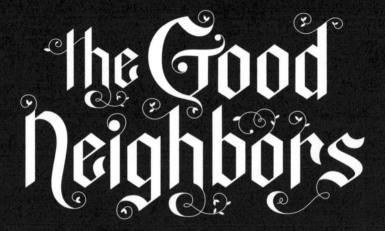

This book was originally published in hardcover by Graphix in 2010.

ISBN 978-0-439-85567-9

10 9 8 7 6 5 4 3 2 1 11 12 13 14 15

First Scholastic paperback printing, October 2011
"Good Neighbors" title lettering by Jessica Hische
Lettering by John Green
Edited by David Levithan
Book design by Phil Falco
Creative Director: David Saylor
Printed in the U.S.A. 23

the Good Neighbors

BY

HOLLY BLACK
& TED NAIFEH

book three
KIND

graphix

New York   Toronto   London   Auckland   Sydney   Mexico City   New Delhi   Hong Kong

WHAT DO YOU DO AFTER
THE END OF THE WORLD?

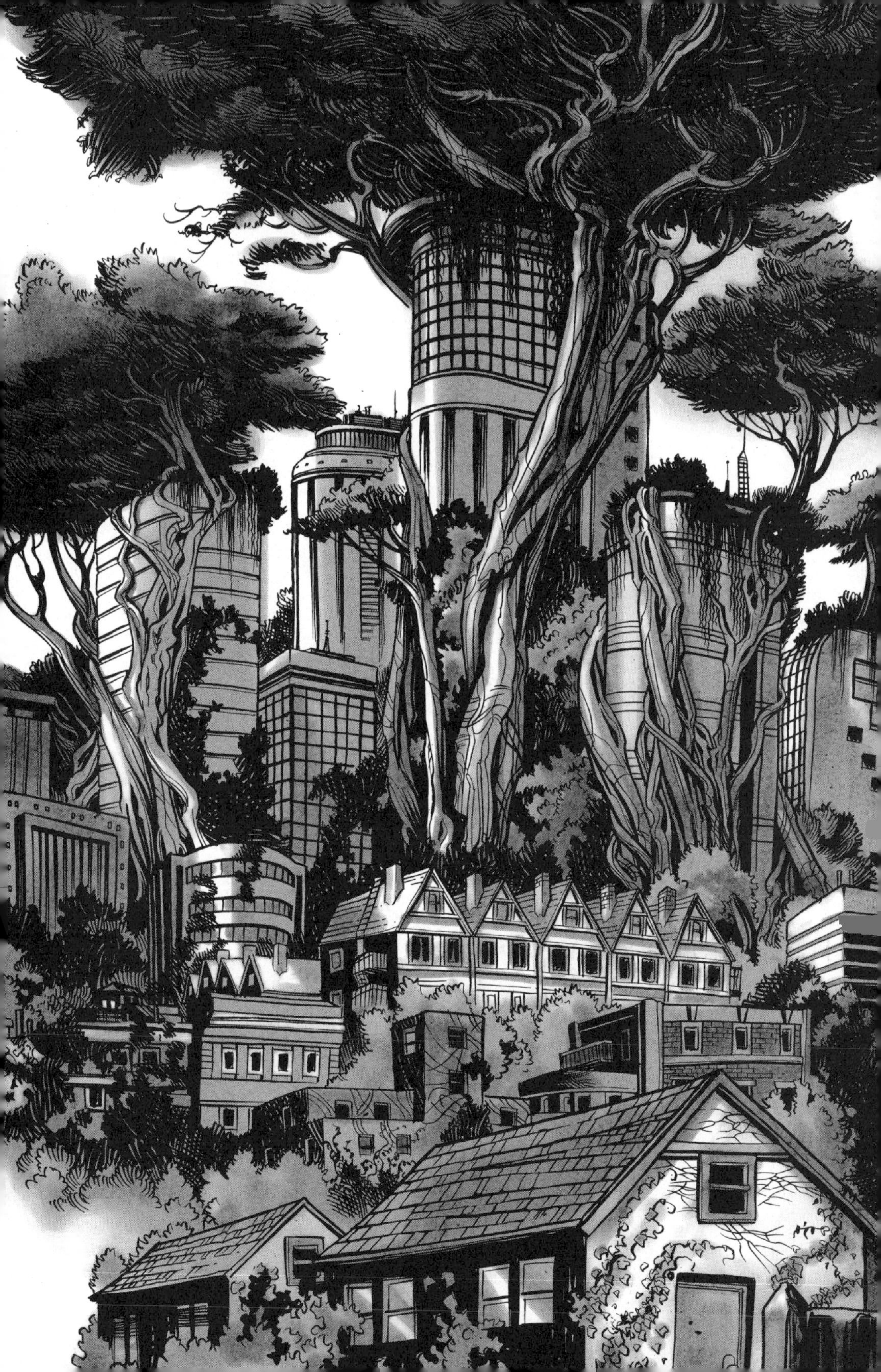

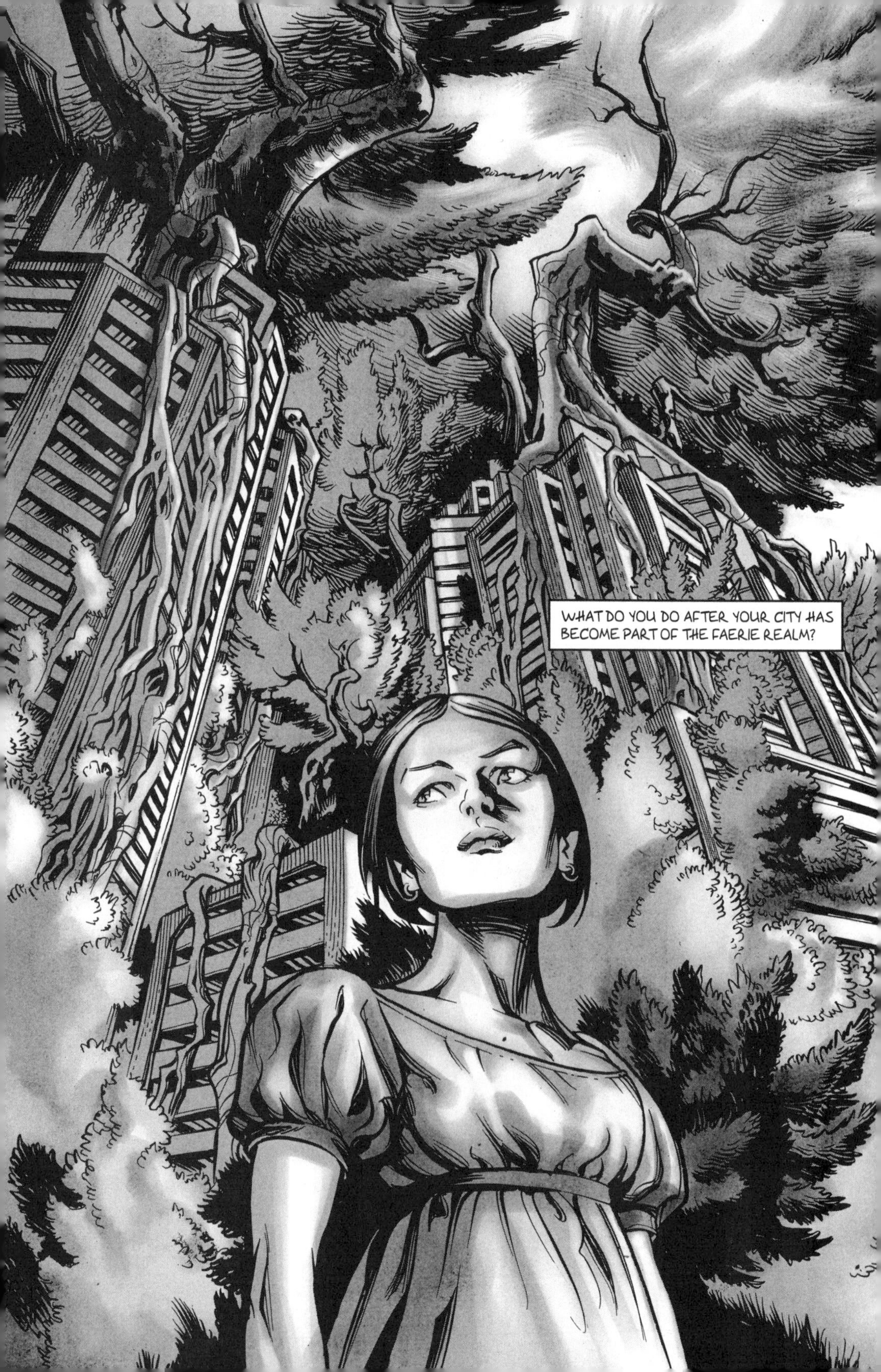
WHAT DO YOU DO AFTER YOUR CITY HAS BECOME PART OF THE FAERIE REALM?

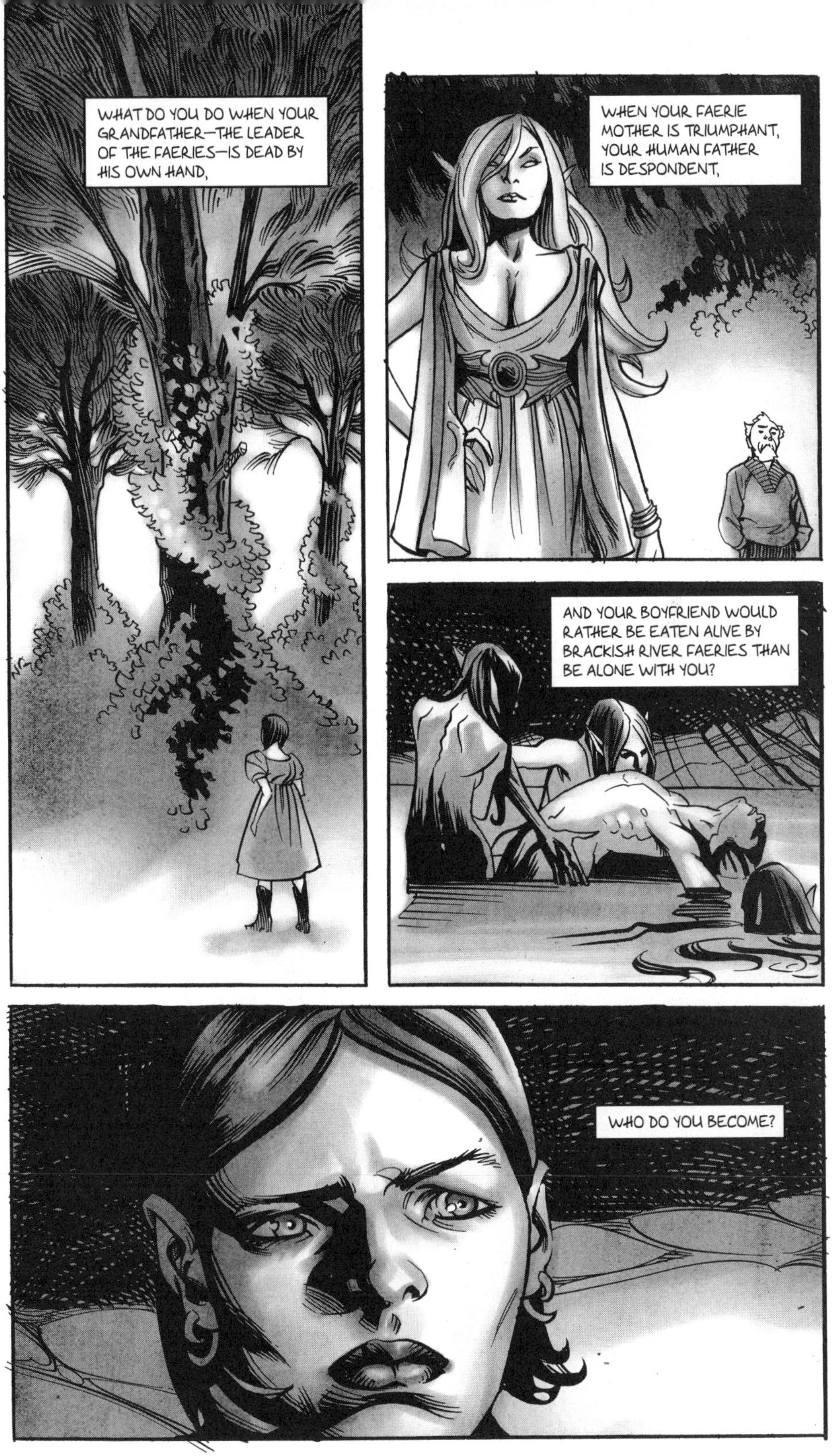
WHAT DO YOU DO WHEN YOUR GRANDFATHER—THE LEADER OF THE FAERIES—IS DEAD BY HIS OWN HAND,
WHEN YOUR FAERIE MOTHER IS TRIUMPHANT, YOUR HUMAN FATHER IS DESPONDENT,
AND YOUR BOYFRIEND WOULD RATHER BE EATEN ALIVE BY BRACKISH RIVER FAERIES THAN BE ALONE WITH YOU?
WHO DO YOU BECOME?

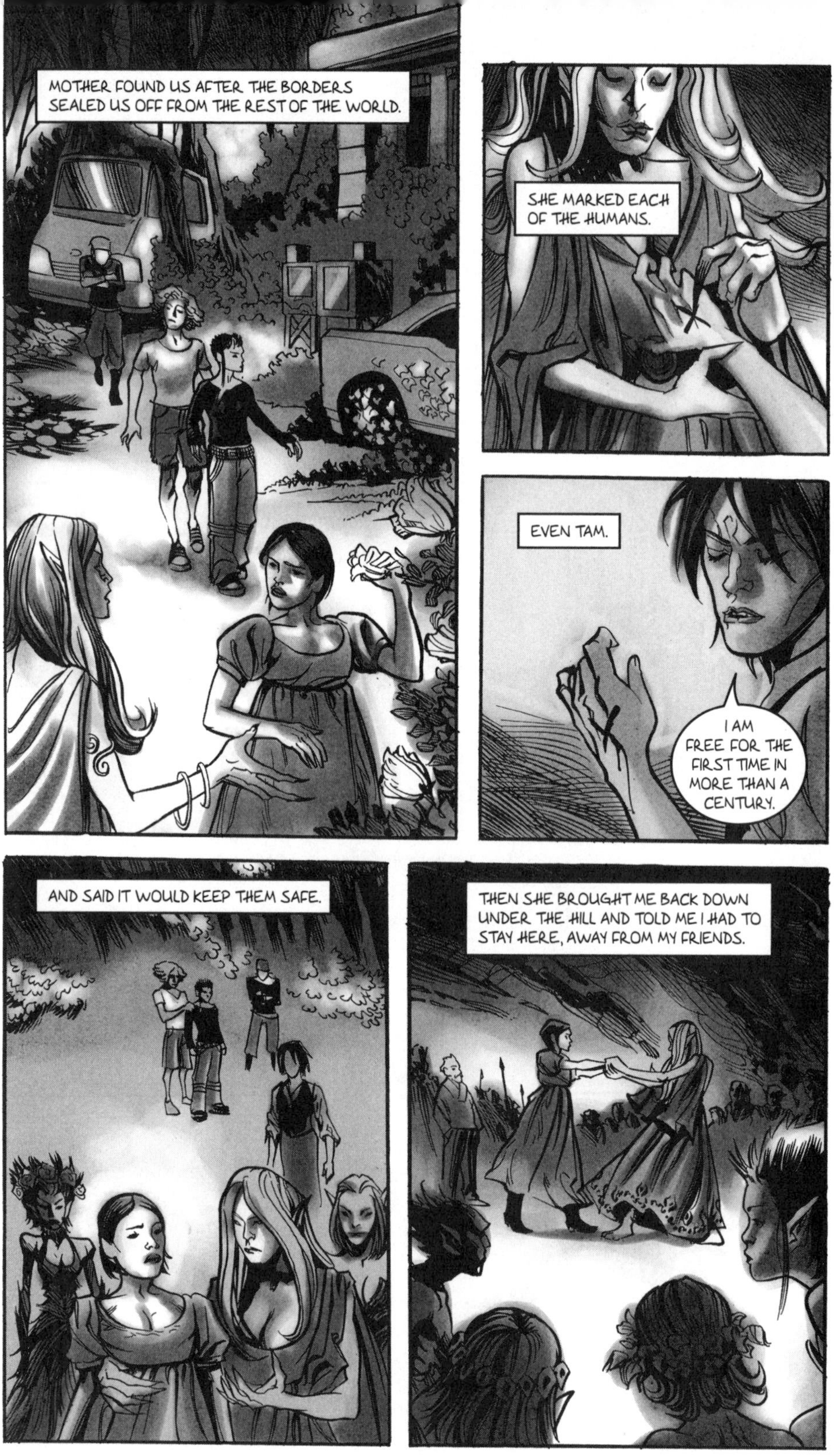
MOTHER FOUND US AFTER THE BORDERS SEALED US OFF FROM THE REST OF THE WORLD.
SHE MARKED EACH OF THE HUMANS.
EVEN TAM.
I AM FREE FOR THE FIRST TIME IN MORE THAN A CENTURY.
AND SAID IT WOULD KEEP THEM SAFE.
THEN SHE BROUGHT ME BACK DOWN UNDER THE HILL AND TOLD ME I HAD TO STAY HERE, AWAY FROM MY FRIENDS.

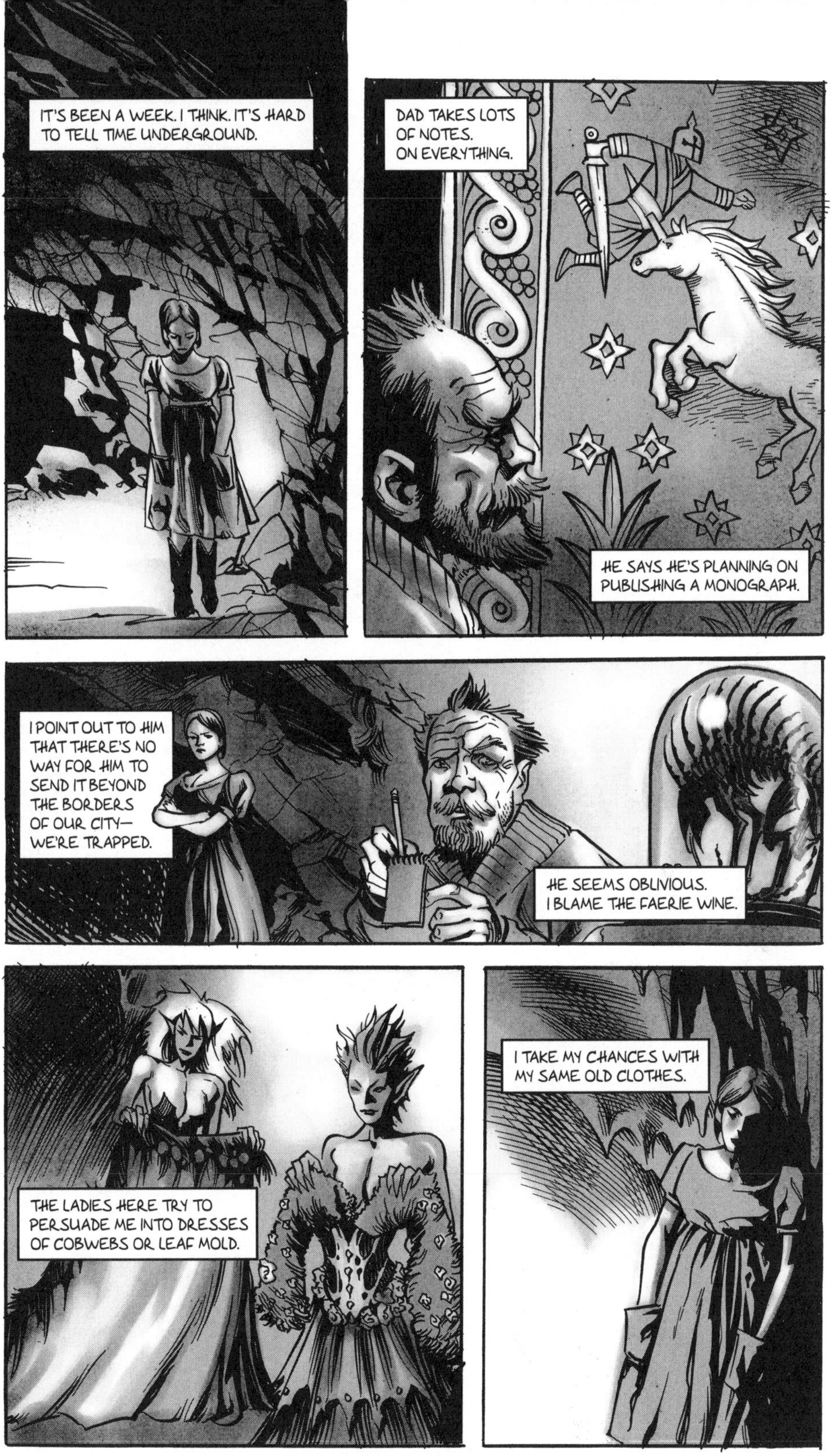
IT'S BEEN A WEEK. I THINK. IT'S HARD TO TELL TIME UNDERGROUND.
DAD TAKES LOTS OF NOTES. ON EVERYTHING.
HE SAYS HE'S PLANNING ON PUBLISHING A MONOGRAPH.
I POINT OUT TO HIM THAT THERE'S NO WAY FOR HIM TO SEND IT BEYOND THE BORDERS OF OUR CITY— WE'RE TRAPPED.
HE SEEMS OBLIVIOUS. I BLAME THE FAERIE WINE.
THE LADIES HERE TRY TO PERSUADE ME INTO DRESSES OF COBWEBS OR LEAF MOLD.
I TAKE MY CHANCES WITH MY SAME OLD CLOTHES.

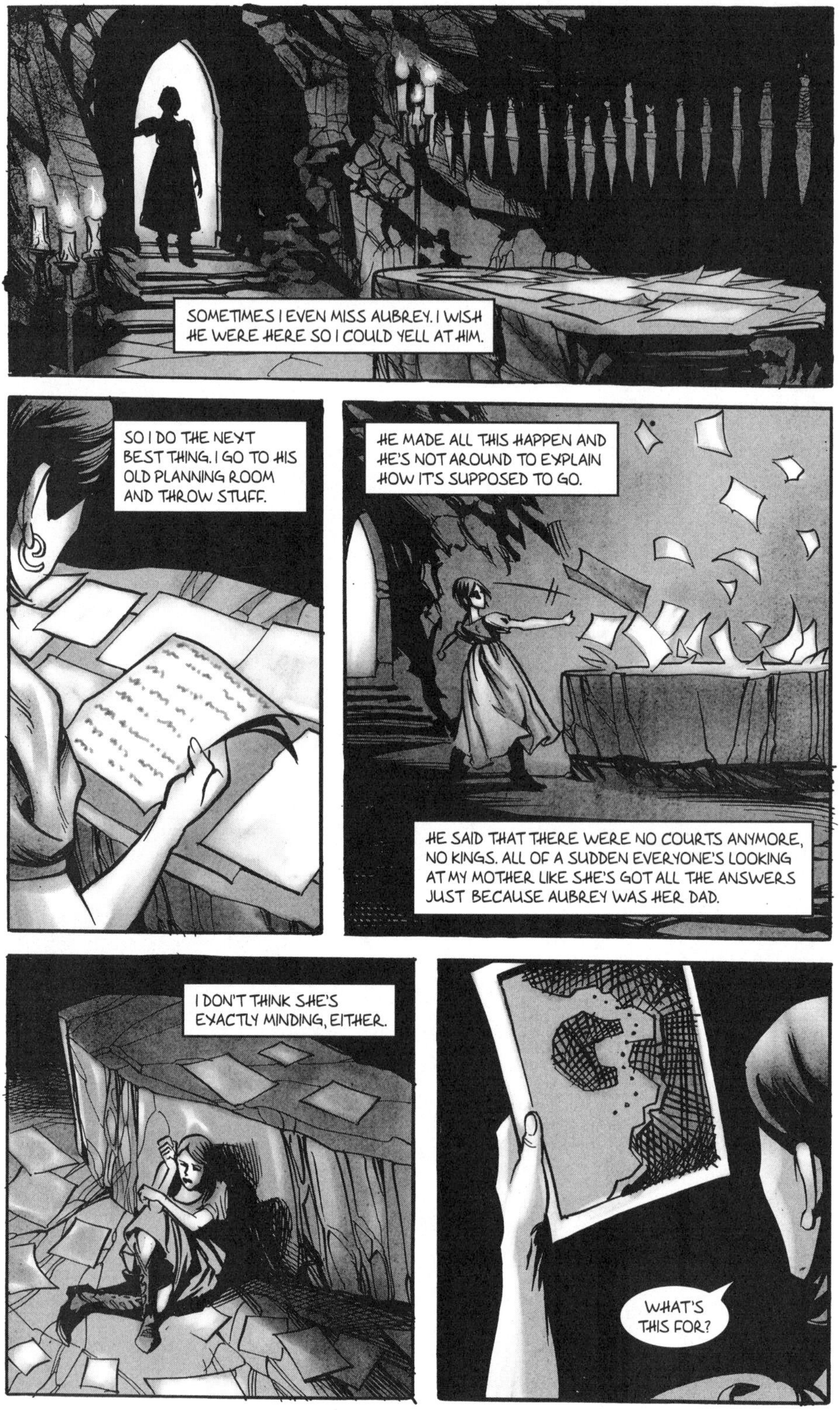
SOMETIMES I EVEN MISS AUBREY. I WISH HE WERE HERE SO I COULD YELL AT HIM.
SO I DO THE NEXT BEST THING. I GO TO HIS OLD PLANNING ROOM AND THROW STUFF.
HE MADE ALL THIS HAPPEN AND HE'S NOT AROUND TO EXPLAIN HOW IT'S SUPPOSED TO GO.
HE SAID THAT THERE WERE NO COURTS ANYMORE, NO KINGS. ALL OF A SUDDEN EVERYONE'S LOOKING AT MY MOTHER LIKE SHE'S GOT ALL THE ANSWERS JUST BECAUSE AUBREY WAS HER DAD.
I DON'T THINK SHE'S EXACTLY MINDING, EITHER.
WHAT'S THIS FOR?

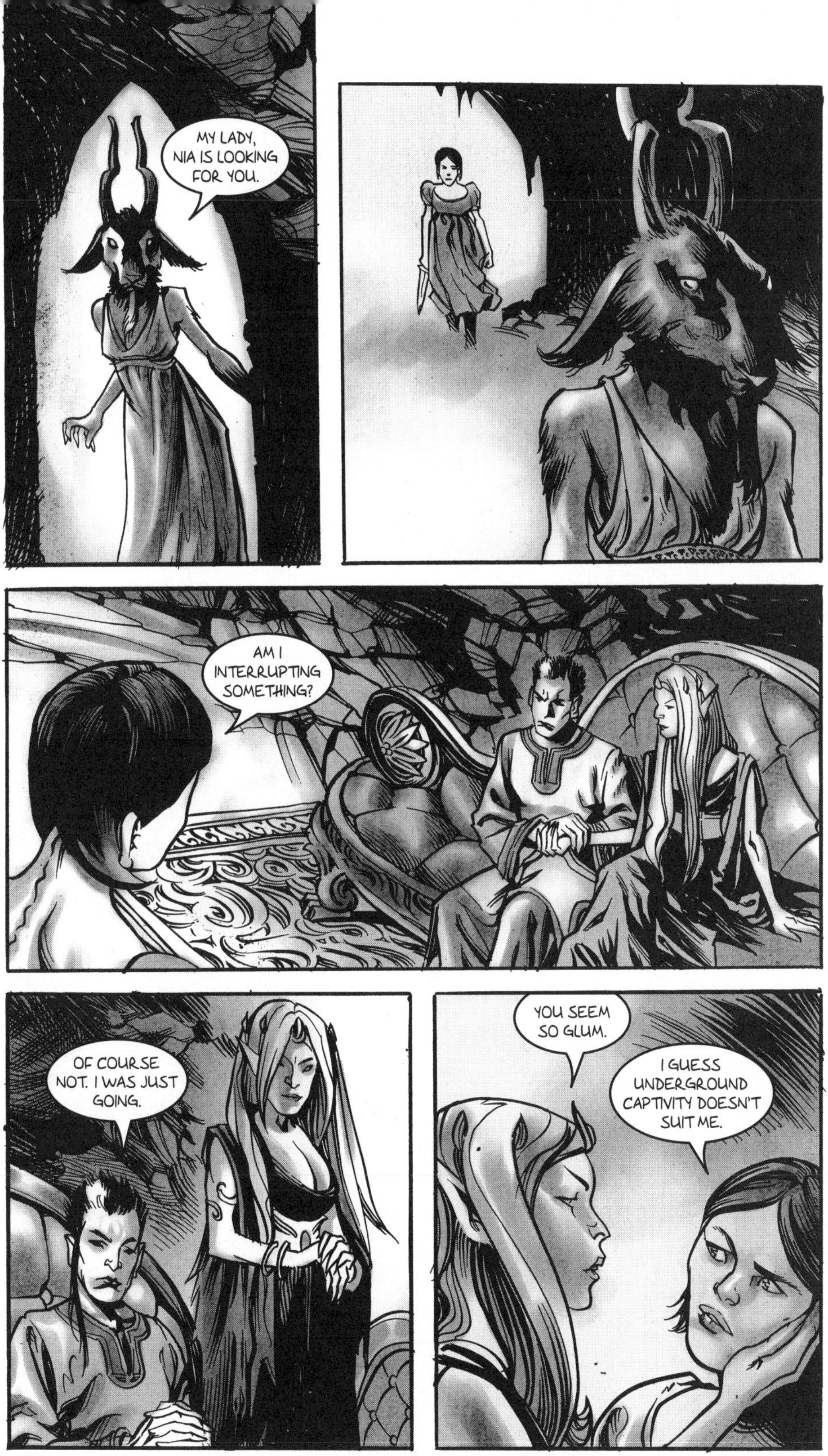

MY LADY, NIA IS LOOKING FOR YOU.
AM I INTERRUPTING SOMETHING?
OF COURSE NOT. I WAS JUST GOING.
YOU SEEM SO GLUM.
I GUESS UNDERGROUND CAPTIVITY DOESN'T SUIT ME.

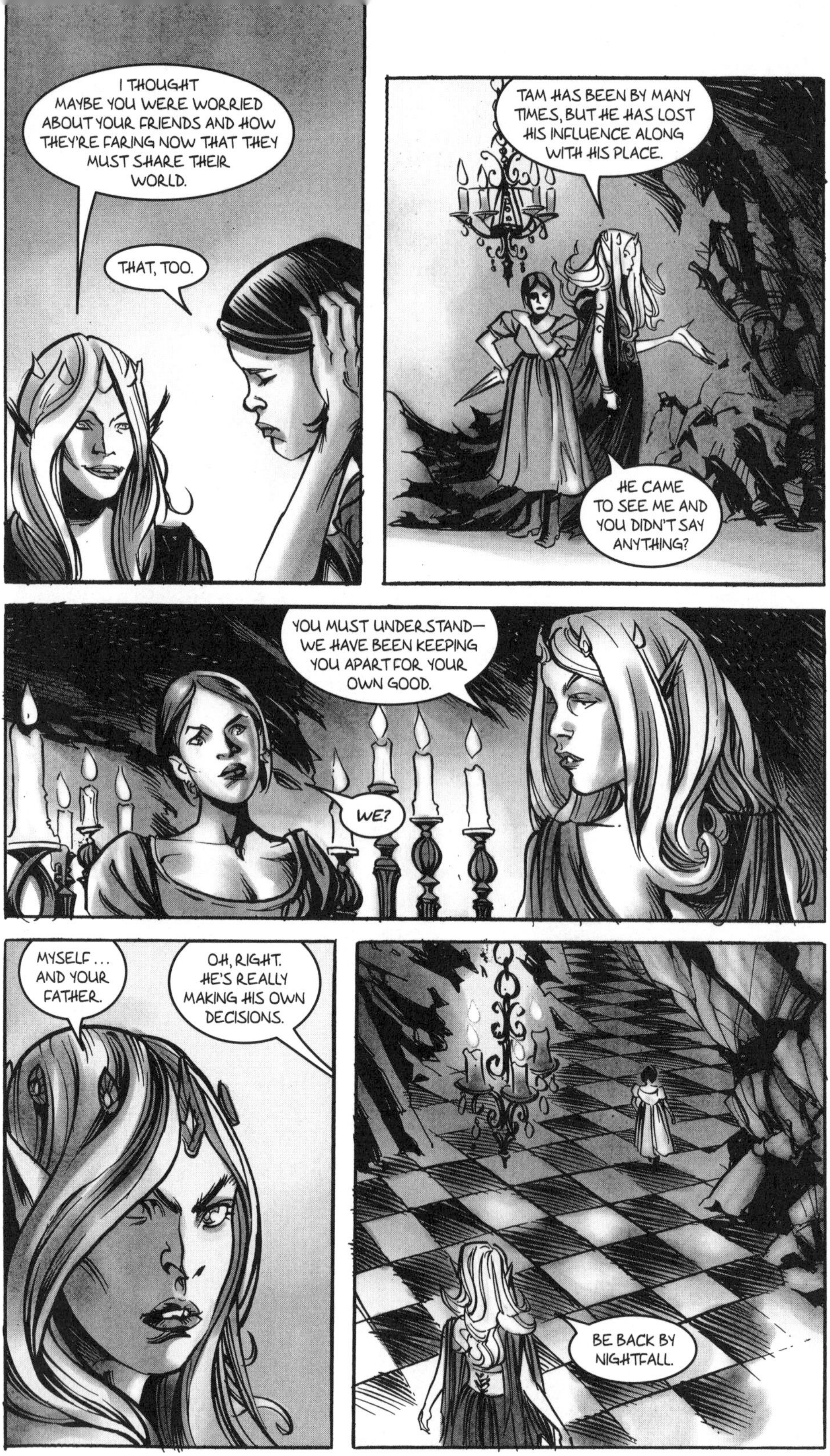
I THOUGHT MAYBE YOU WERE WORRIED ABOUT YOUR FRIENDS AND HOW THEY'RE FARING NOW THAT THEY MUST SHARE THEIR WORLD.
THAT, TOO.
TAM HAS BEEN BY MANY TIMES, BUT HE HAS LOST HIS INFLUENCE ALONG WITH HIS PLACE.
HE CAME TO SEE ME AND YOU DIDN'T SAY ANYTHING?
YOU MUST UNDERSTAND— WE HAVE BEEN KEEPING YOU APART FOR YOUR OWN GOOD.
WE?
MYSELF . . . AND YOUR FATHER.
OH, RIGHT. HE'S REALLY MAKING HIS OWN DECISIONS.
BE BACK BY NIGHTFALL.

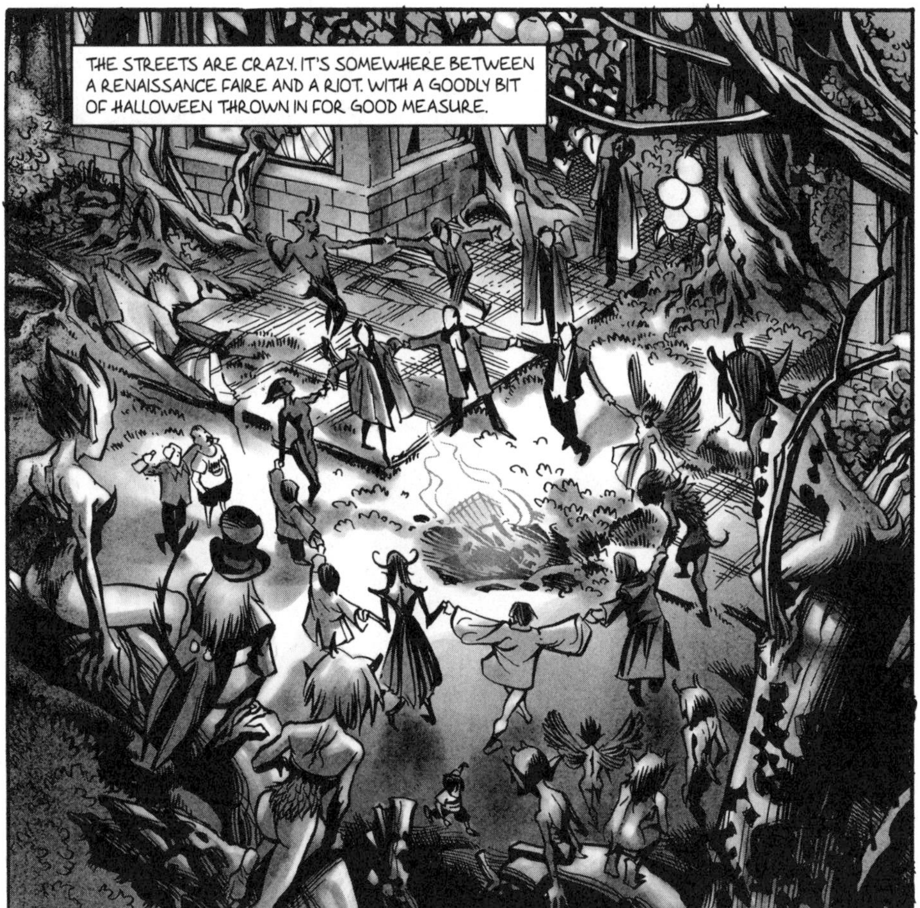
THE STREETS ARE CRAZY. IT'S SOMEWHERE BETWEEN A RENAISSANCE FAIRE AND A RIOT. WITH A GOODLY BIT OF HALLOWEEN THROWN IN FOR GOOD MEASURE.

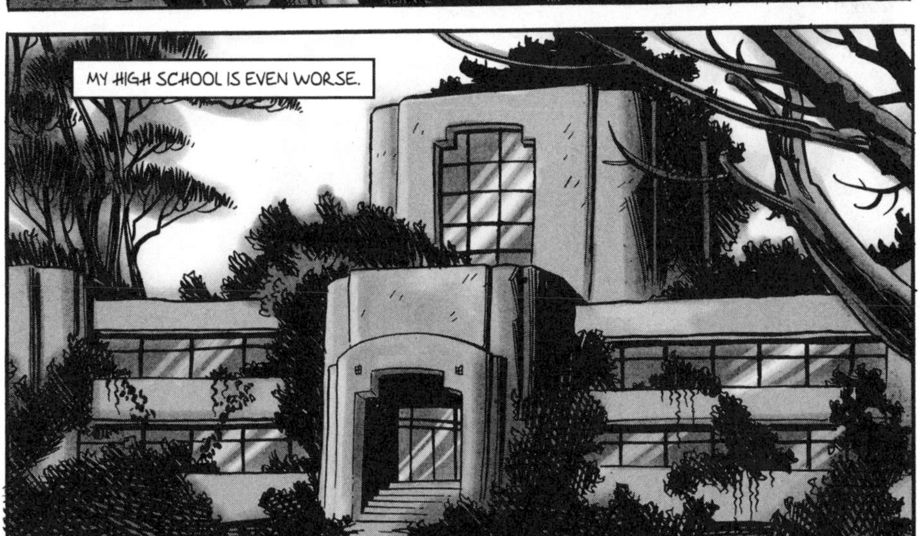
MY HIGH SCHOOL IS EVEN WORSE.

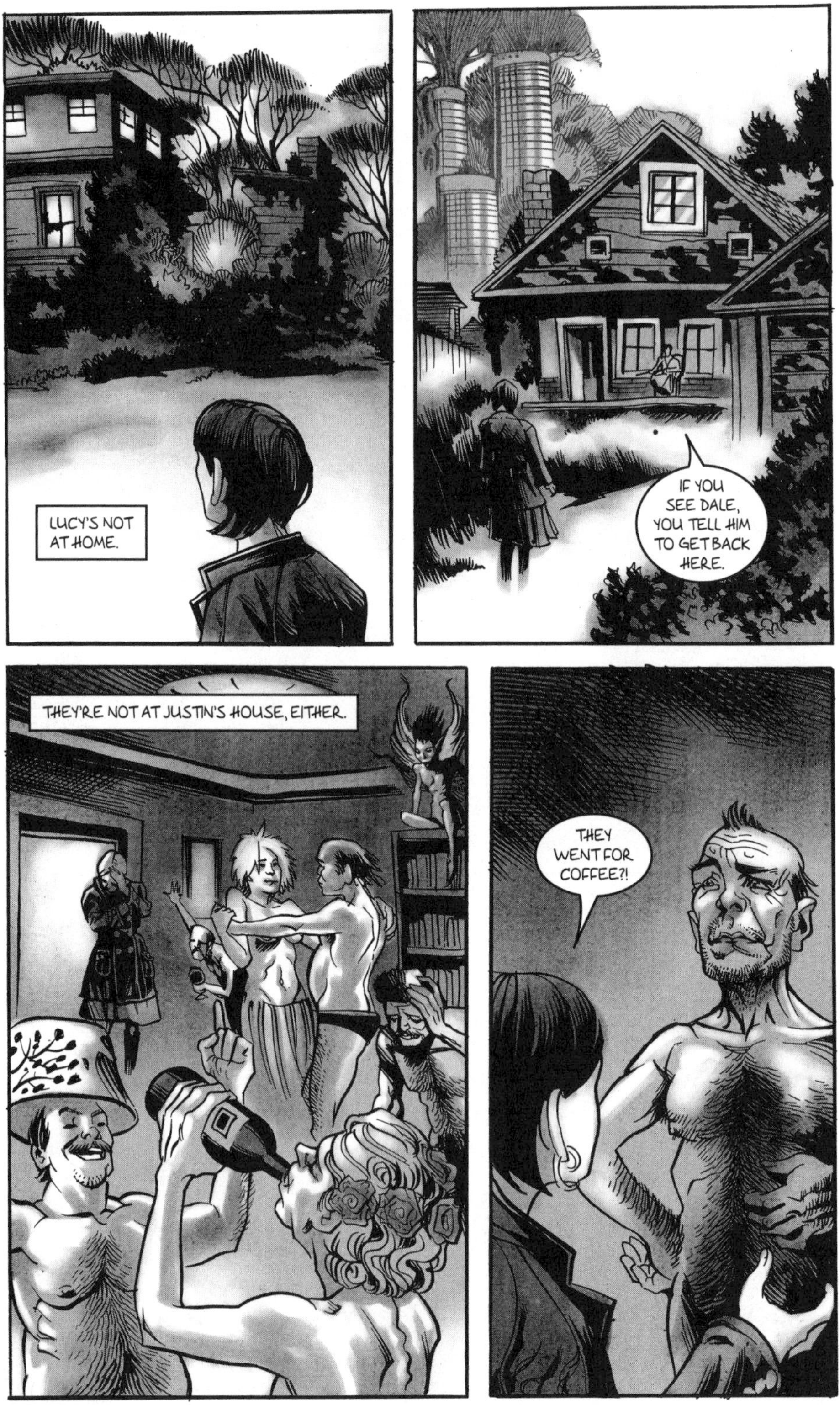
LUCY'S NOT AT HOME.
IF YOU SEE DALE, YOU TELL HIM TO GET BACK HERE.
THEY'RE NOT AT JUSTIN'S HOUSE, EITHER.
THEY WENT FOR COFFEE?!

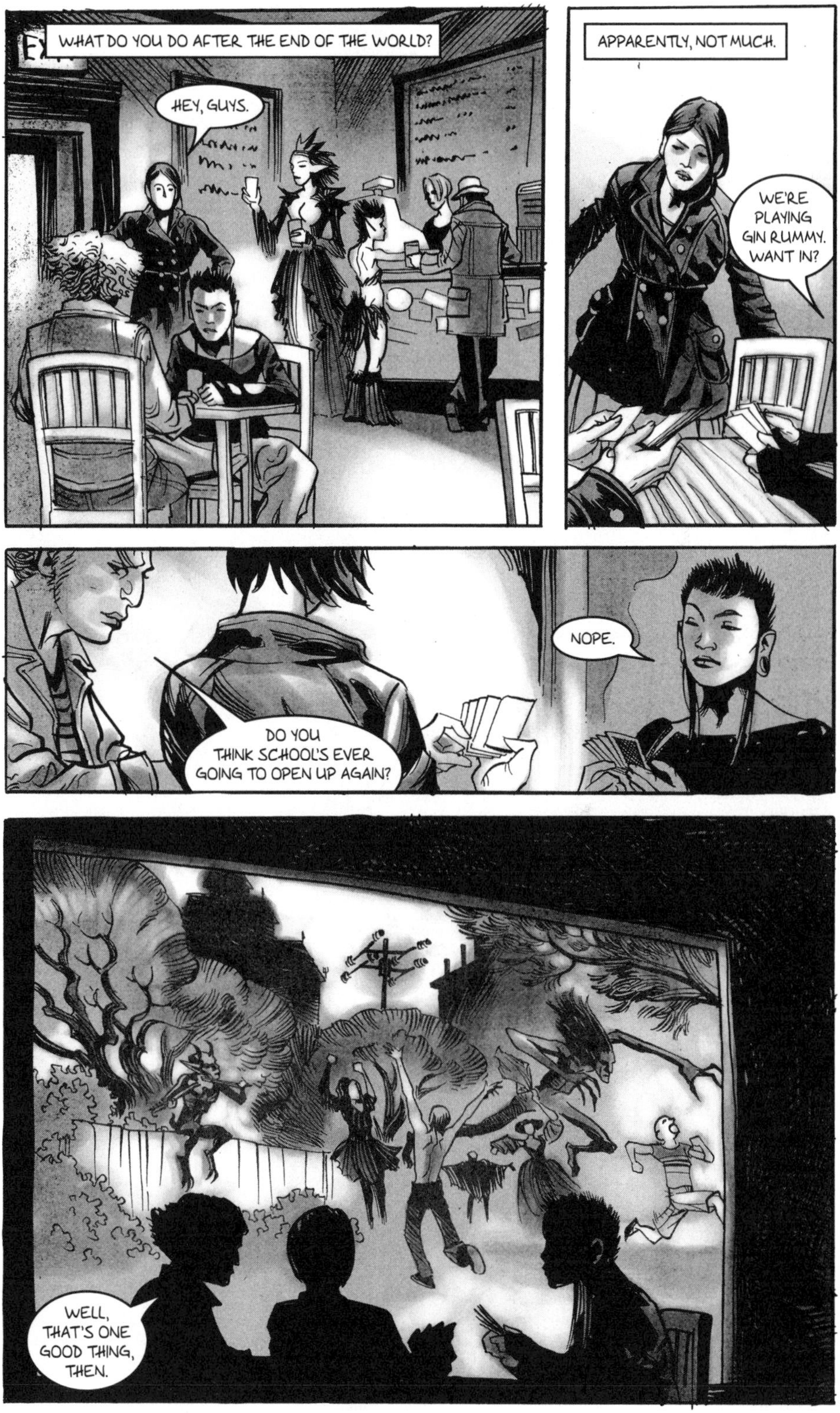
WHAT DO YOU DO AFTER THE END OF THE WORLD?
HEY, GUYS.
APPARENTLY, NOT MUCH.
WE'RE PLAYING GIN RUMMY. WANT IN?
DO YOU THINK SCHOOL'S EVER GOING TO OPEN UP AGAIN?
NOPE.
WELL, THAT'S ONE GOOD THING, THEN.

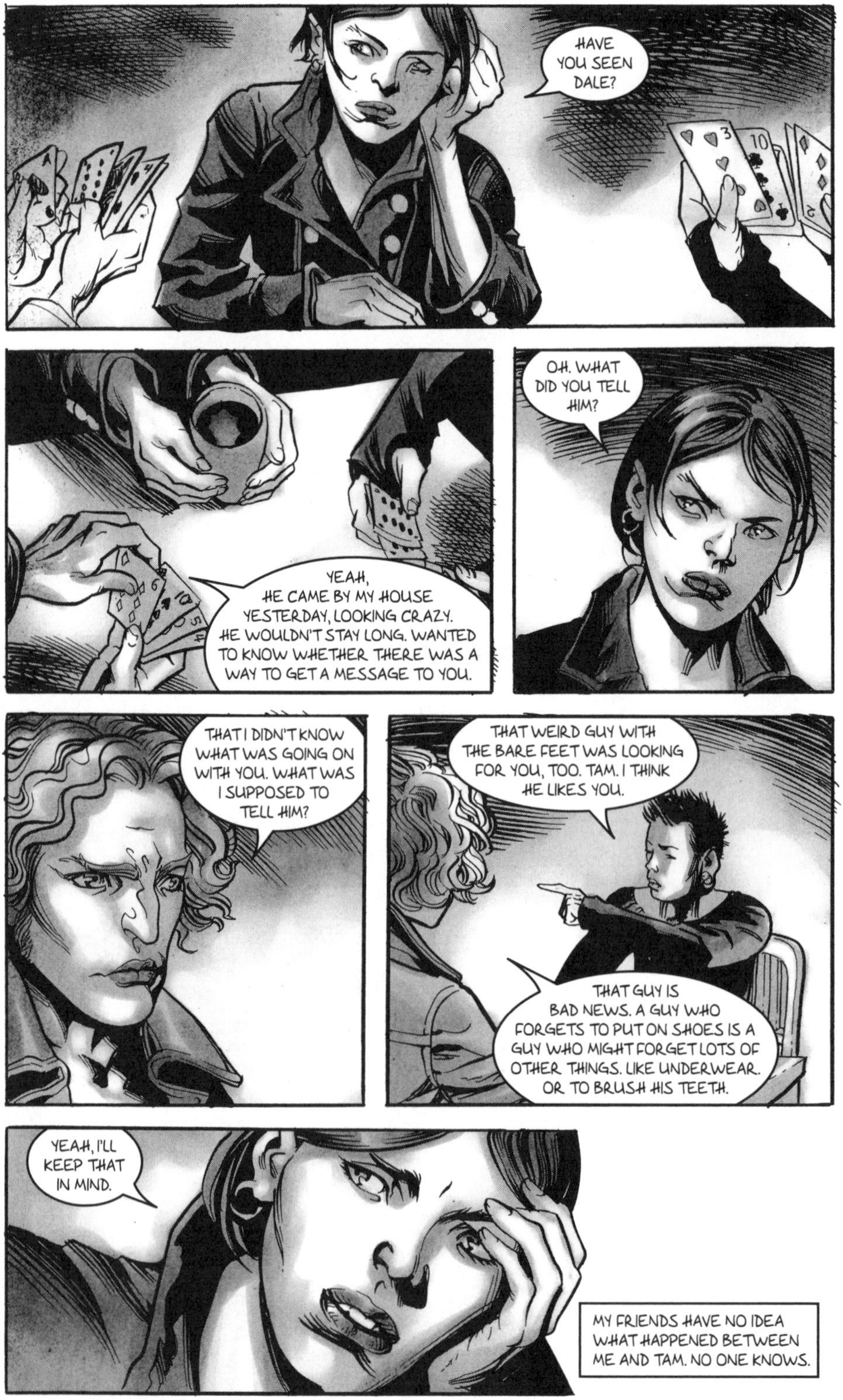
HAVE YOU SEEN DALE?
YEAH, HE CAME BY MY HOUSE YESTERDAY, LOOKING CRAZY. HE WOULDN'T STAY LONG. WANTED TO KNOW WHETHER THERE WAS A WAY TO GET A MESSAGE TO YOU.
OH. WHAT DID YOU TELL HIM?
THAT I DIDN'T KNOW WHAT WAS GOING ON WITH YOU. WHAT WAS I SUPPOSED TO TELL HIM?
THAT WEIRD GUY WITH THE BARE FEET WAS LOOKING FOR YOU, TOO. TAM. I THINK HE LIKES YOU.
THAT GUY IS BAD NEWS. A GUY WHO FORGETS TO PUT ON SHOES IS A GUY WHO MIGHT FORGET LOTS OF OTHER THINGS. LIKE UNDERWEAR. OR TO BRUSH HIS TEETH.
YEAH, I'LL KEEP THAT IN MIND.
MY FRIENDS HAVE NO IDEA WHAT HAPPENED BETWEEN ME AND TAM. NO ONE KNOWS.

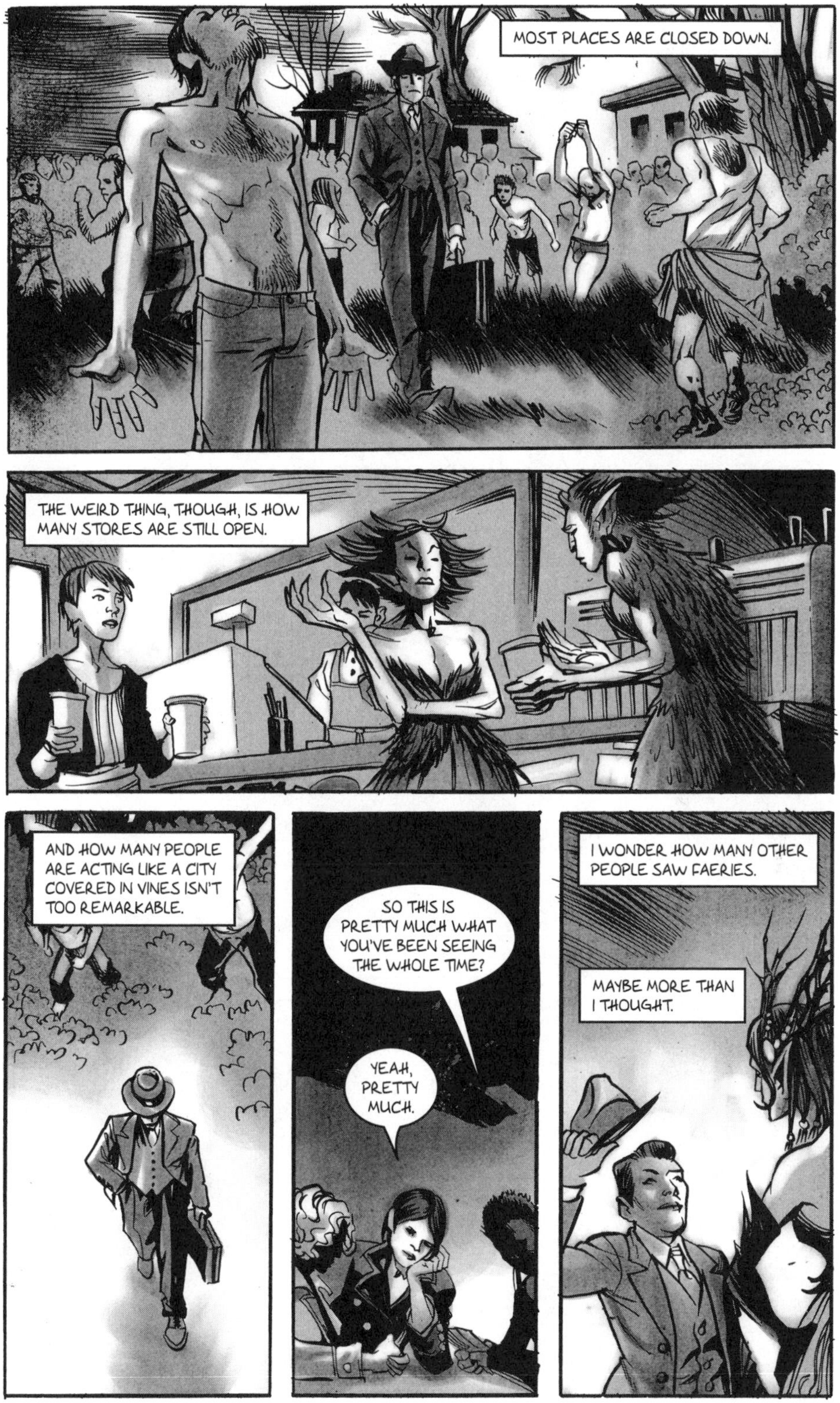

MOST PLACES ARE CLOSED DOWN.
THE WEIRD THING, THOUGH, IS HOW MANY STORES ARE STILL OPEN.
AND HOW MANY PEOPLE ARE ACTING LIKE A CITY COVERED IN VINES ISN'T TOO REMARKABLE.
SO THIS IS PRETTY MUCH WHAT YOU'VE BEEN SEEING THE WHOLE TIME?
YEAH, PRETTY MUCH.
I WONDER HOW MANY OTHER PEOPLE SAW FAERIES.
MAYBE MORE THAN I THOUGHT.

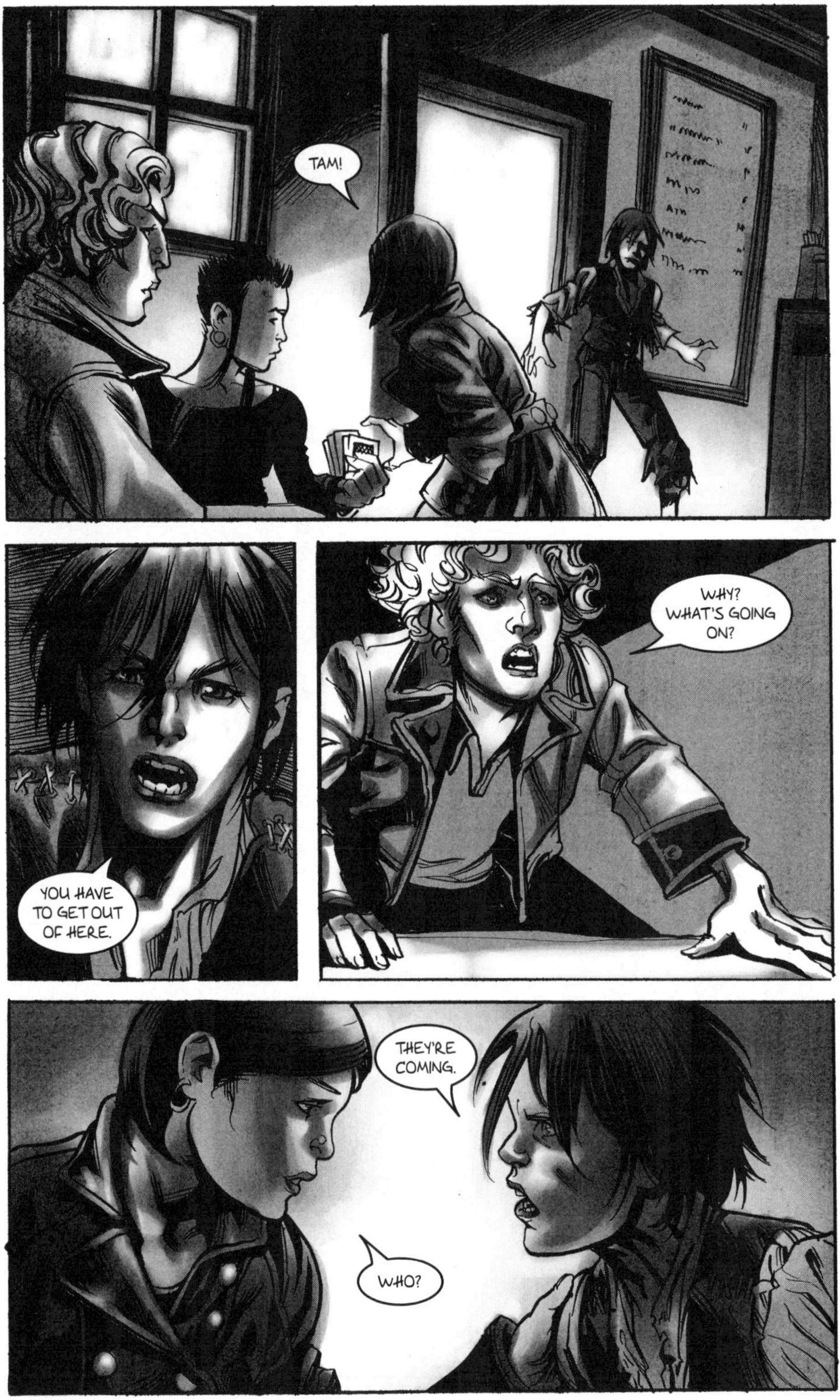
TAM!
YOU HAVE TO GET OUT OF HERE.
WHY? WHAT'S GOING ON?
THEY'RE COMING.
WHO?

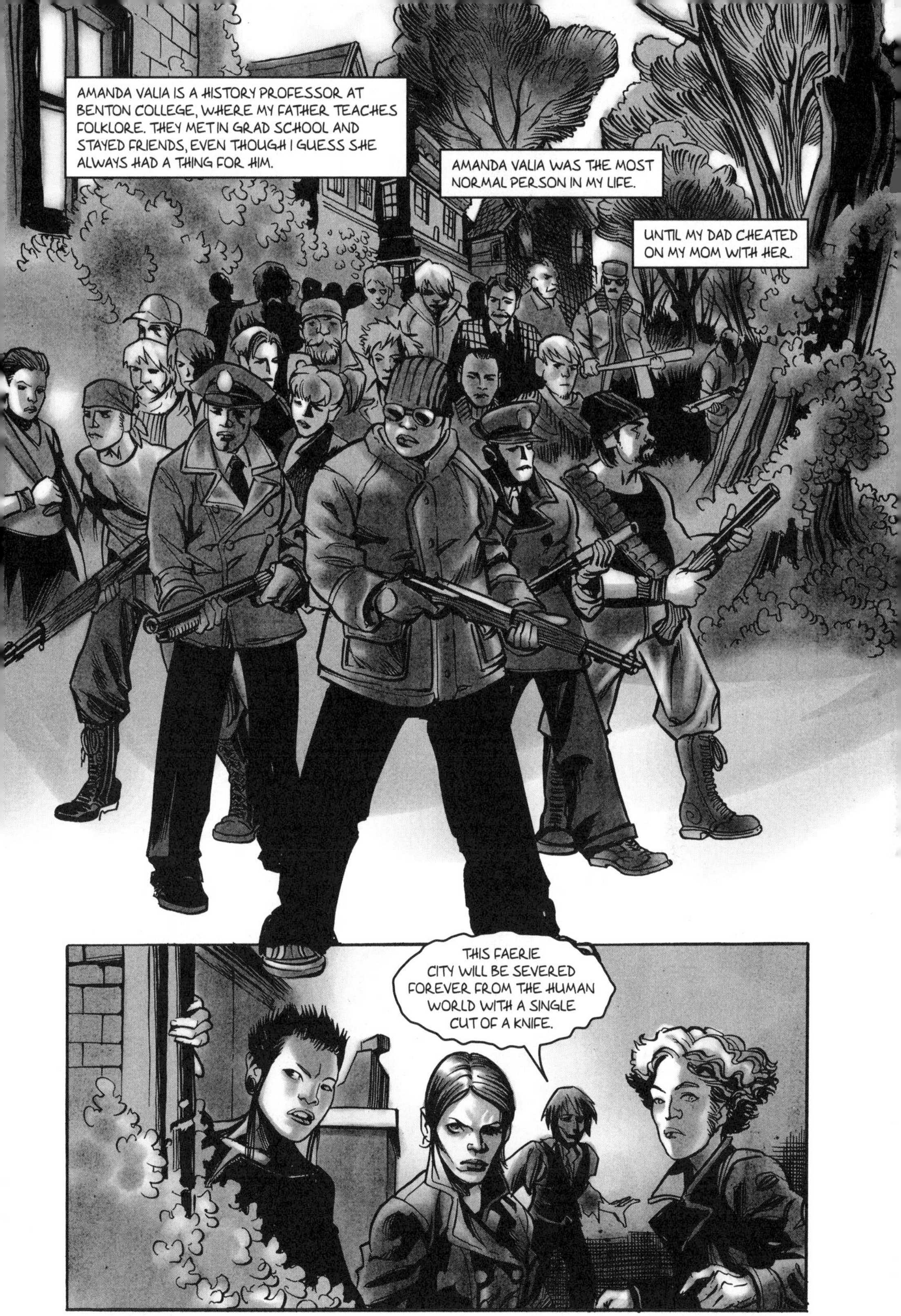
AMANDA VALIA IS A HISTORY PROFESSOR AT BENTON COLLEGE, WHERE MY FATHER TEACHES FOLKLORE. THEY MET IN GRAD SCHOOL AND STAYED FRIENDS, EVEN THOUGH I GUESS SHE ALWAYS HAD A THING FOR HIM.
AMANDA VALIA WAS THE MOST NORMAL PERSON IN MY LIFE.
UNTIL MY DAD CHEATED ON MY MOM WITH HER.
THIS FAERIE CITY WILL BE SEVERED FOREVER FROM THE HUMAN WORLD WITH A SINGLE CUT OF A KNIFE.

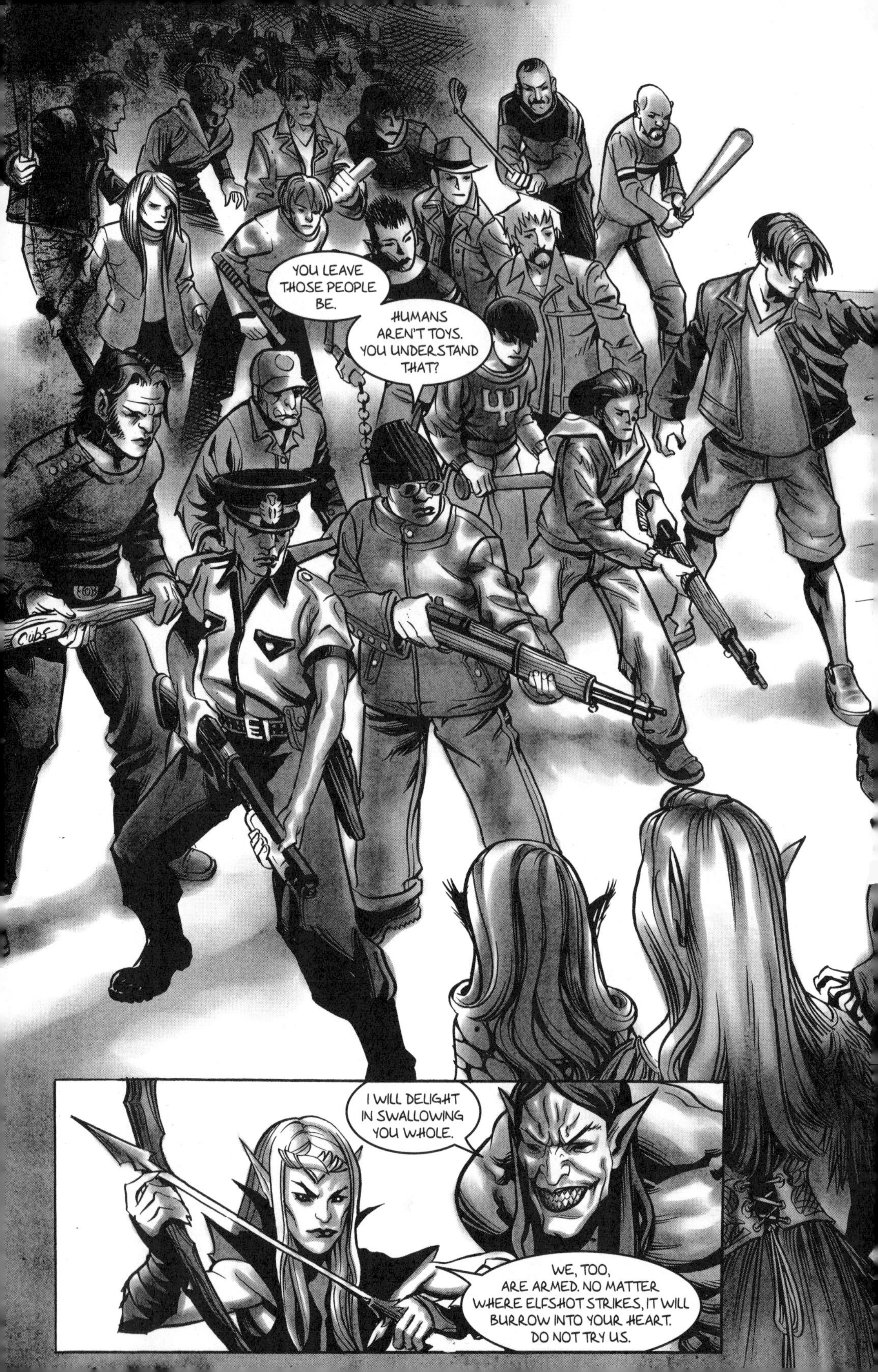
YOU LEAVE THOSE PEOPLE BE.
HUMANS AREN'T TOYS. YOU UNDERSTAND THAT?
Cubs
I WILL DELIGHT IN SWALLOWING YOU WHOLE.
WE, TOO, ARE ARMED. NO MATTER WHERE ELFSHOT STRIKES, IT WILL BURROW INTO YOUR HEART. DO NOT TRY US.

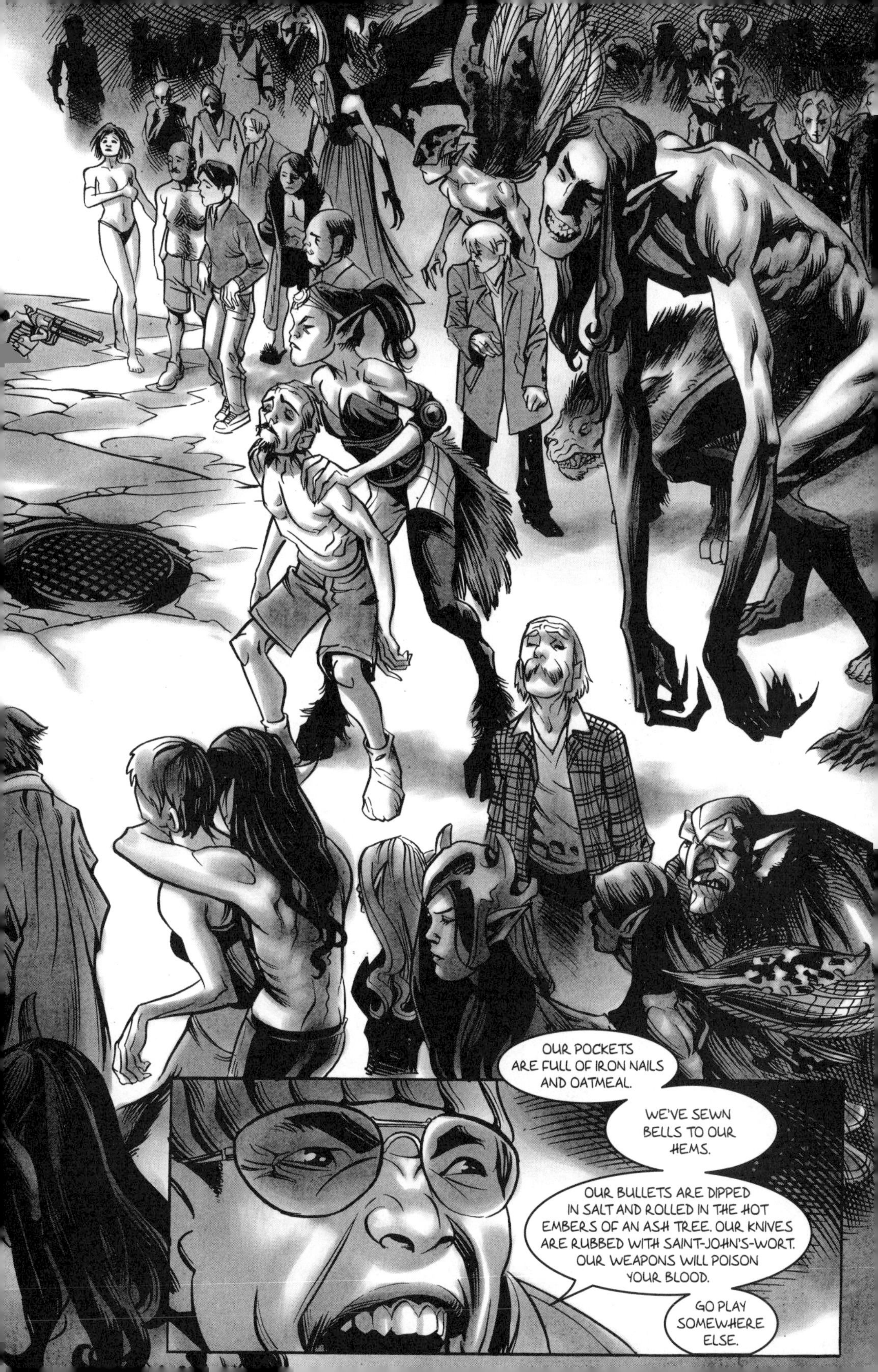
OUR POCKETS ARE FULL OF IRON NAILS AND OATMEAL.
WE'VE SEWN BELLS TO OUR HEMS.
OUR BULLETS ARE DIPPED IN SALT AND ROLLED IN THE HOT EMBERS OF AN ASH TREE. OUR KNIVES ARE RUBBED WITH SAINT-JOHN'S-WORT. OUR WEAPONS WILL POISON YOUR BLOOD.
GO PLAY SOMEWHERE ELSE.

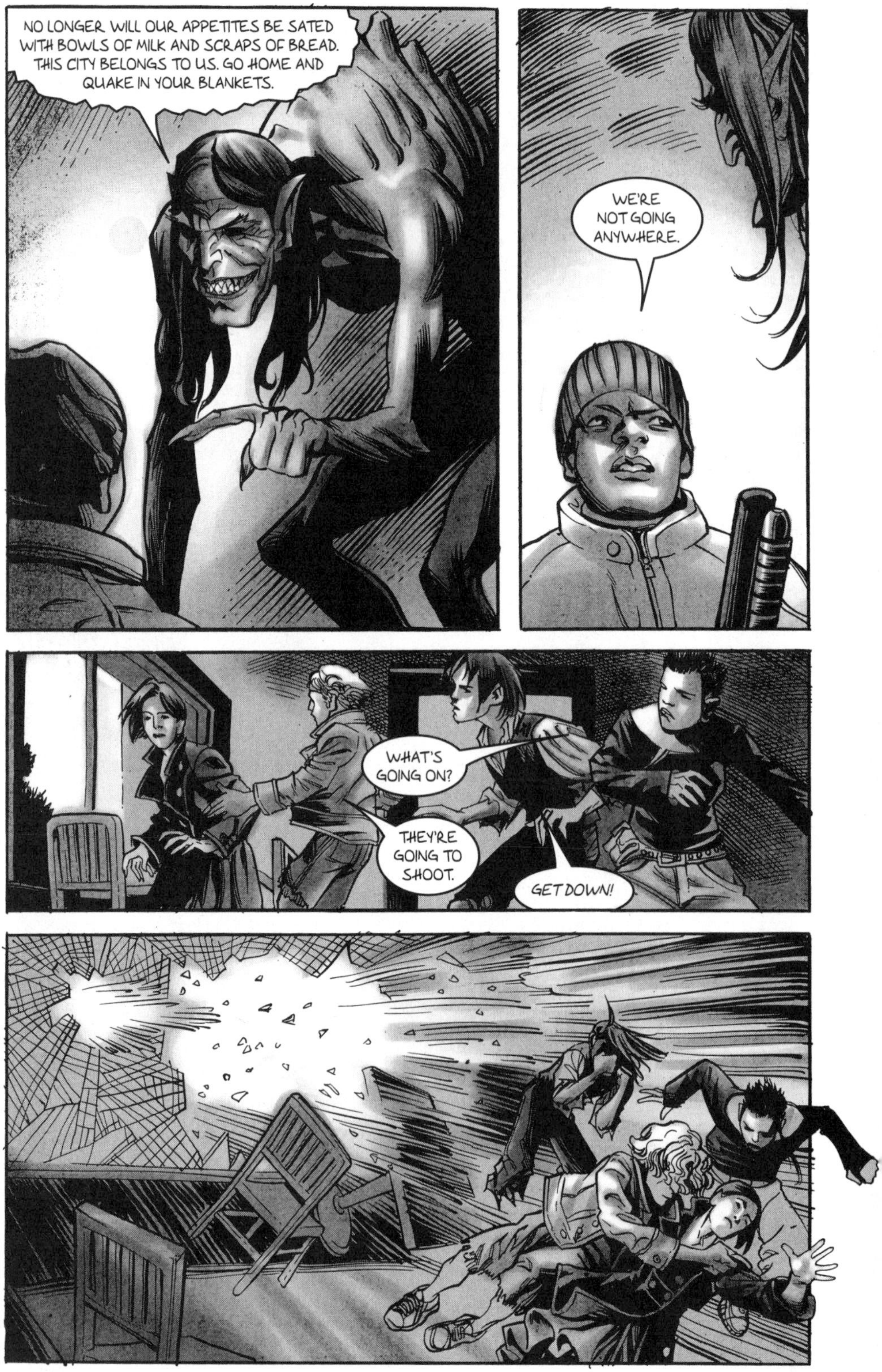
NO LONGER WILL OUR APPETITES BE SATED WITH BOWLS OF MILK AND SCRAPS OF BREAD. THIS CITY BELONGS TO US. GO HOME AND QUAKE IN YOUR BLANKETS.
WE'RE NOT GOING ANYWHERE.
WHAT'S GOING ON?
THEY'RE GOING TO SHOOT.
GET DOWN!

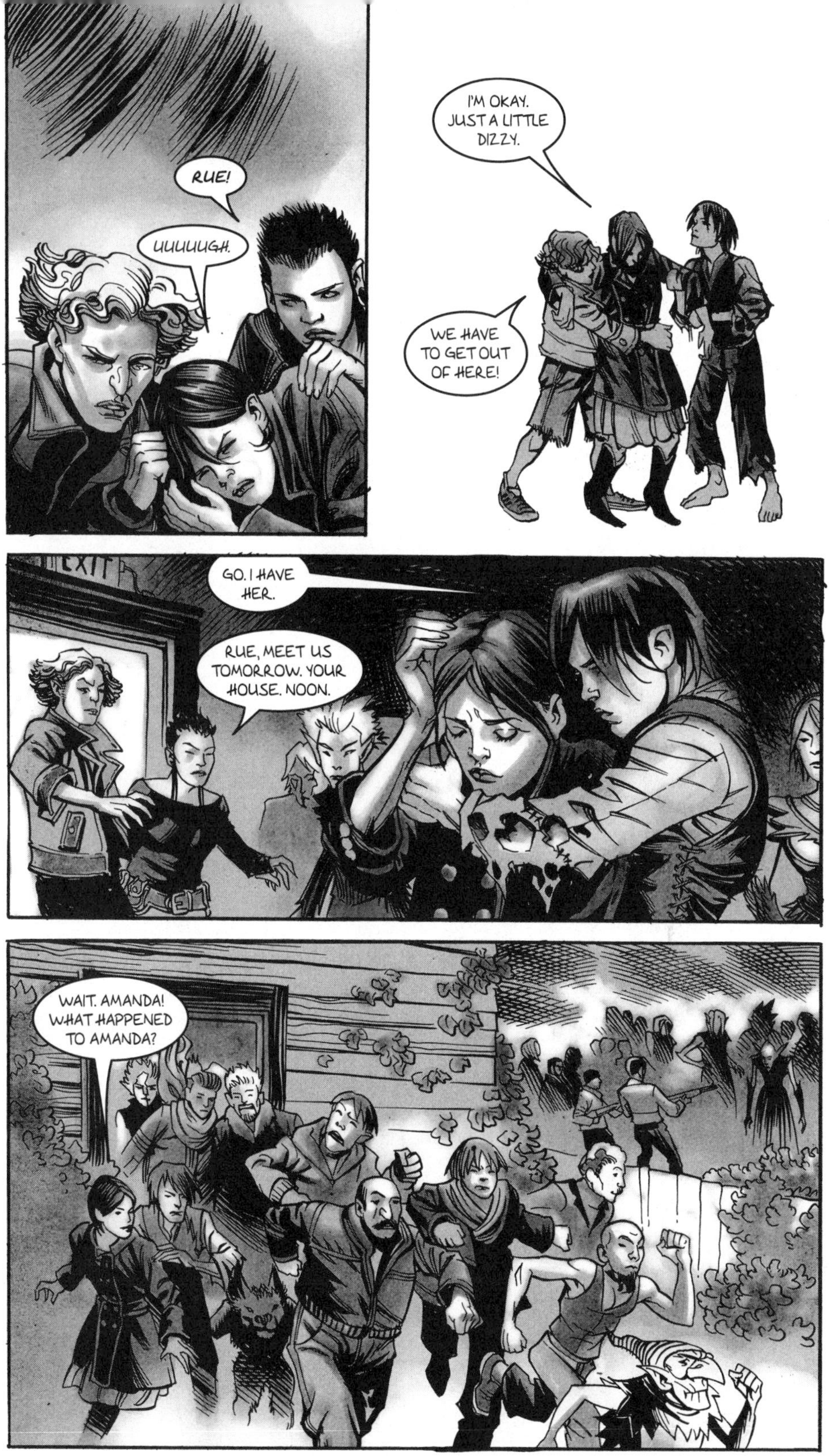
RUE!
UUUUUGH.
I'M OKAY. JUST A LITTLE DIZZY.
WE HAVE TO GET OUT OF HERE!
EXIT
GO. I HAVE HER.
RUE, MEET US TOMORROW. YOUR HOUSE. NOON.
WAIT. AMANDA! WHAT HAPPENED TO AMANDA?

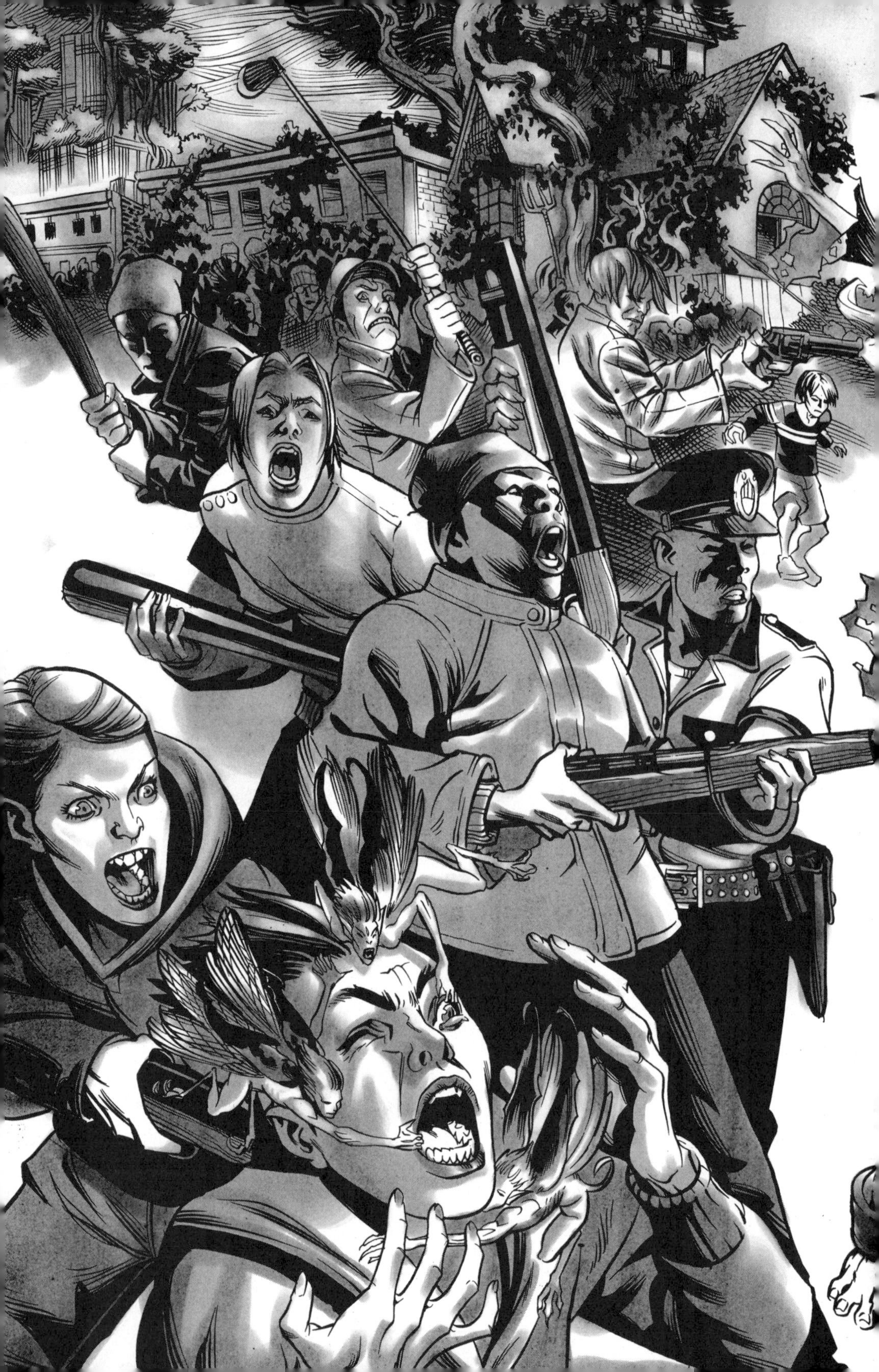

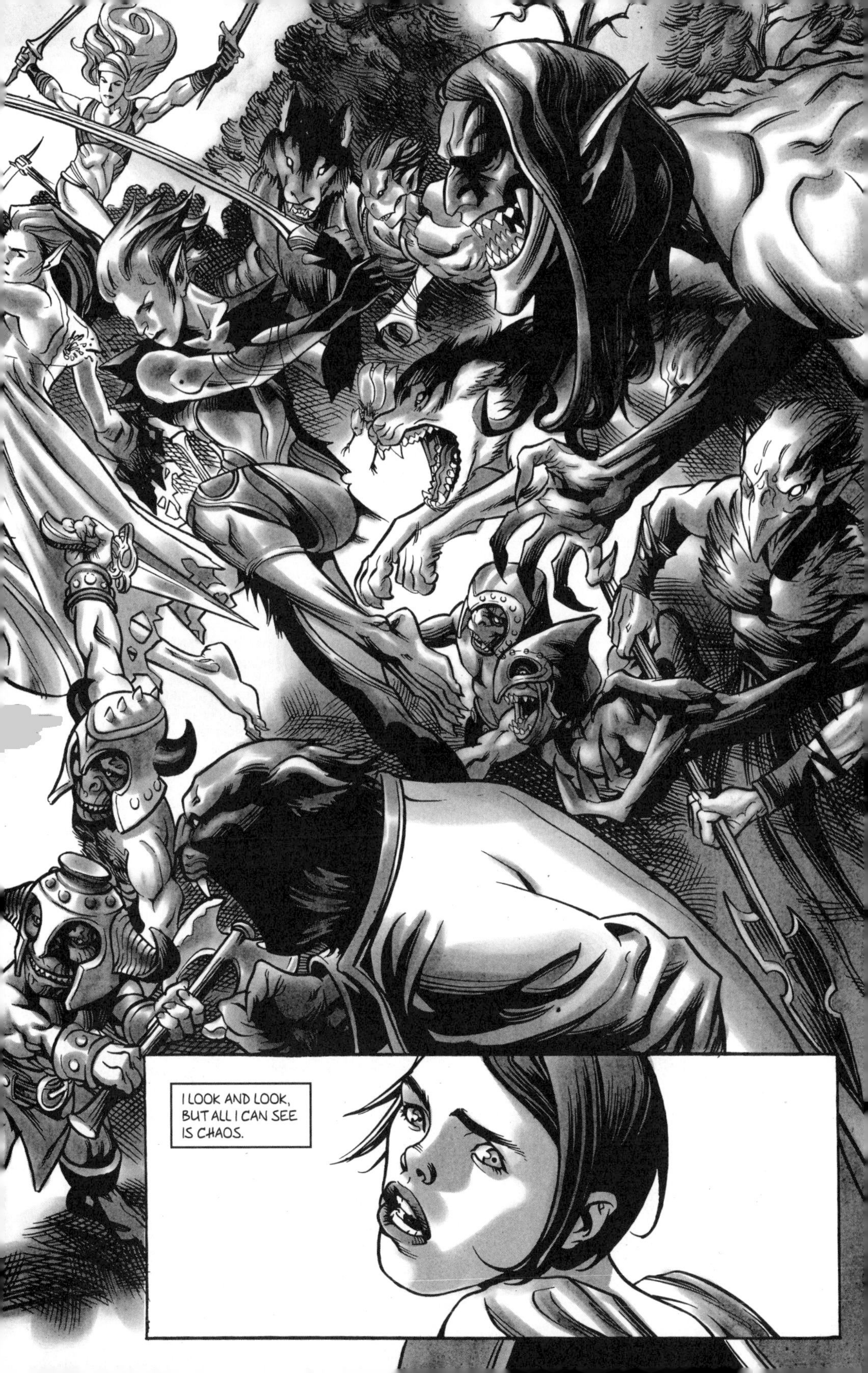
I LOOK AND LOOK, BUT ALL I CAN SEE IS CHAOS.

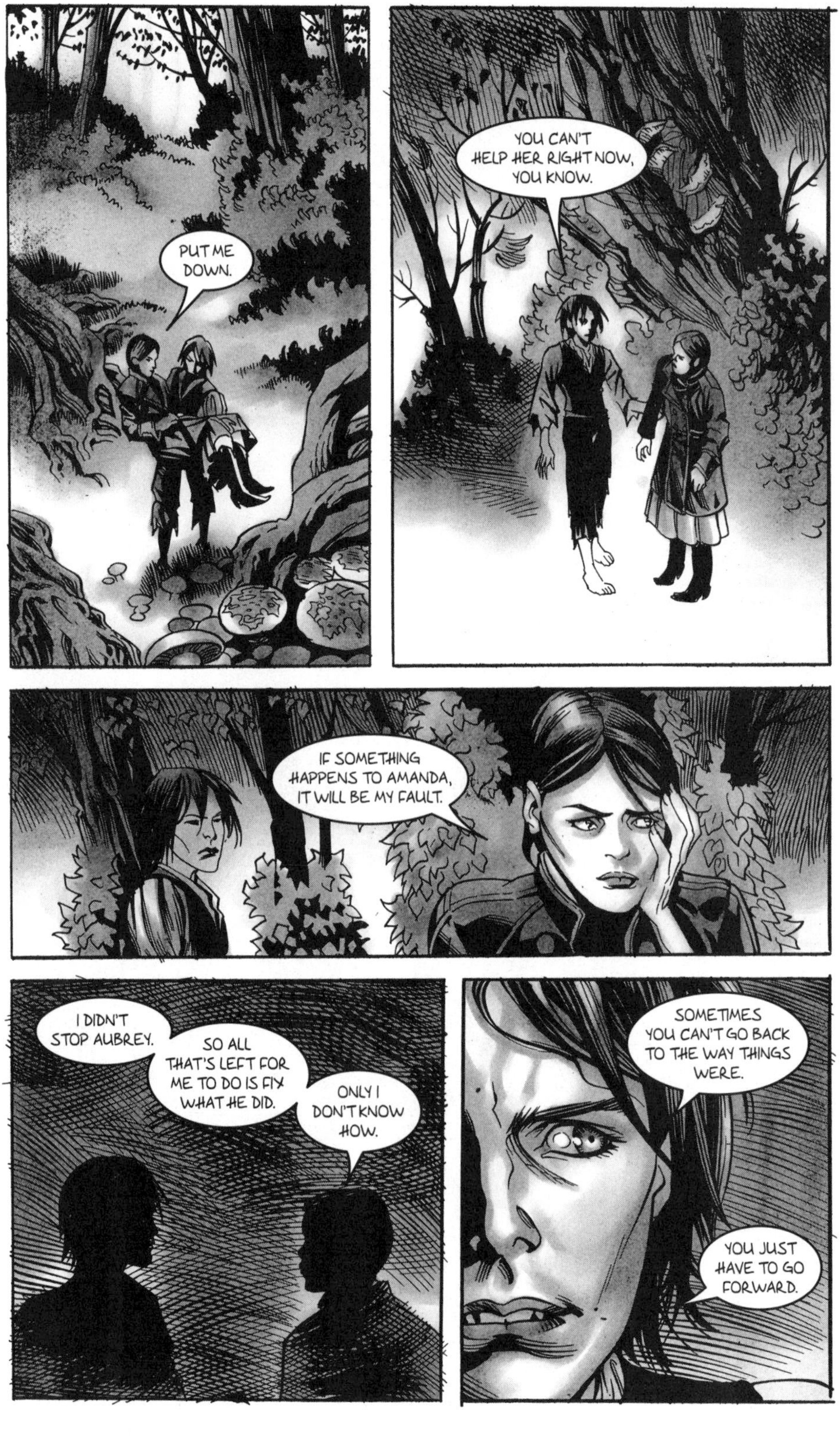
PUT ME DOWN.
YOU CAN'T HELP HER RIGHT NOW, YOU KNOW.
IF SOMETHING HAPPENS TO AMANDA, IT WILL BE MY FAULT.
I DIDN'T STOP AUBREY.
SO ALL THAT'S LEFT FOR ME TO DO IS FIX WHAT HE DID.
ONLY I DON'T KNOW HOW.
SOMETIMES YOU CAN'T GO BACK TO THE WAY THINGS WERE.
YOU JUST HAVE TO GO FORWARD.

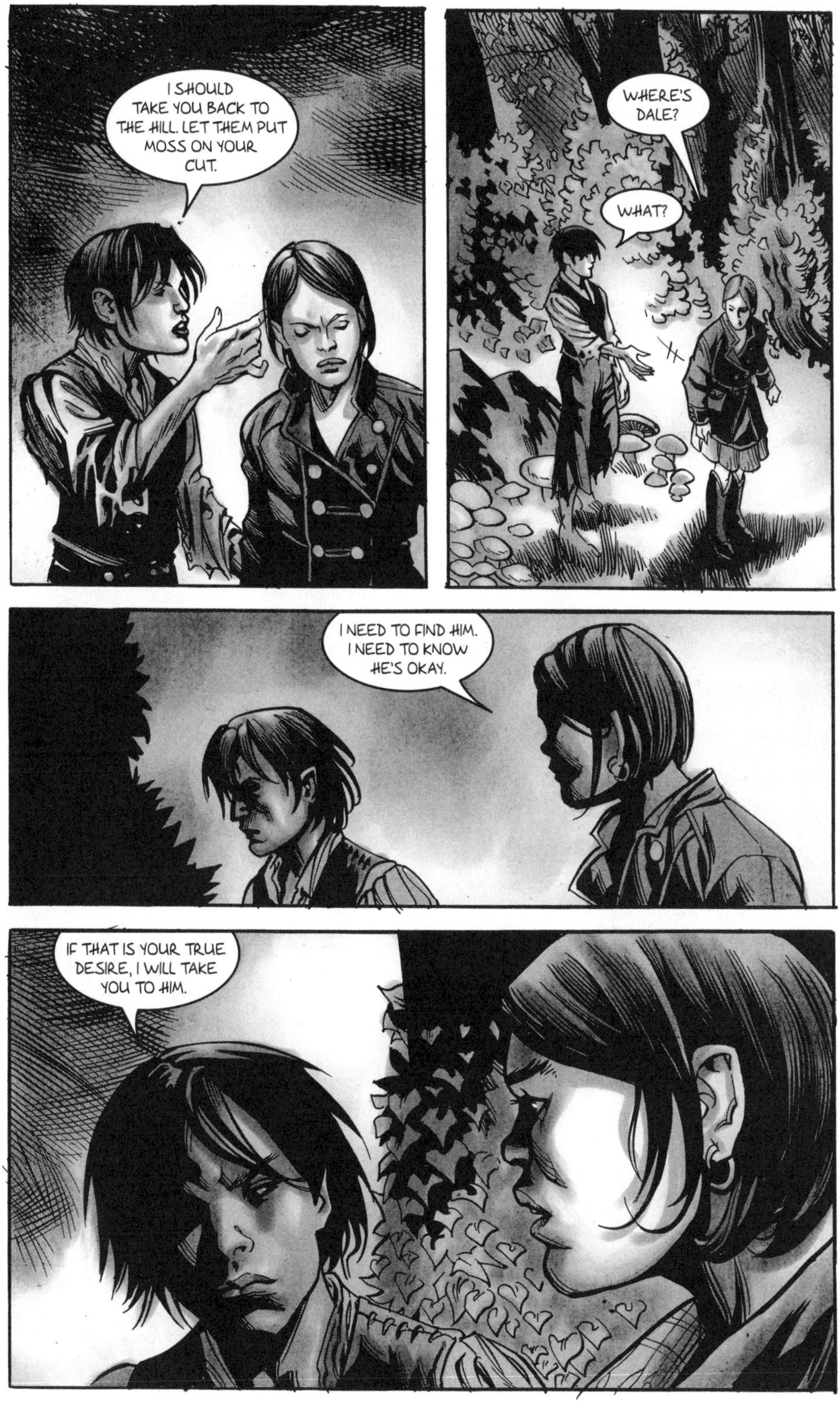
I SHOULD TAKE YOU BACK TO THE HILL. LET THEM PUT MOSS ON YOUR CUT.
WHERE'S DALE?
WHAT?
I NEED TO FIND HIM. I NEED TO KNOW HE'S OKAY.
IF THAT IS YOUR TRUE DESIRE, I WILL TAKE YOU TO HIM.

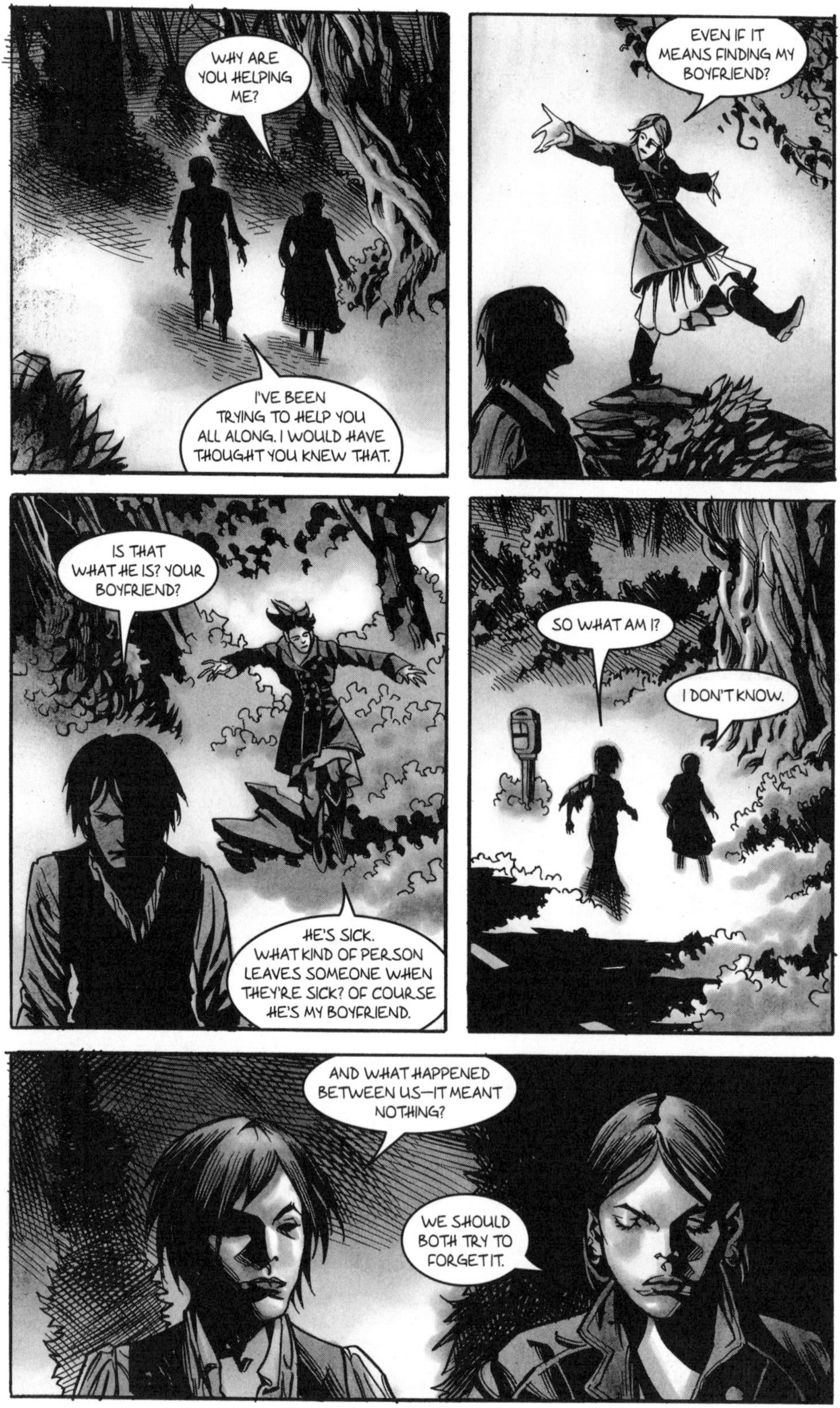
WHY ARE YOU HELPING ME?
I'VE BEEN TRYING TO HELP YOU ALL ALONG. I WOULD HAVE THOUGHT YOU KNEW THAT.
EVEN IF IT MEANS FINDING MY BOYFRIEND?
IS THAT WHAT HE IS? YOUR BOYFRIEND?
HE'S SICK. WHAT KIND OF PERSON LEAVES SOMEONE WHEN THEY'RE SICK? OF COURSE HE'S MY BOYFRIEND.
SO WHAT AM I?
I DON'T KNOW.
AND WHAT HAPPENED BETWEEN US—IT MEANT NOTHING?
WE SHOULD BOTH TRY TO FORGET IT.

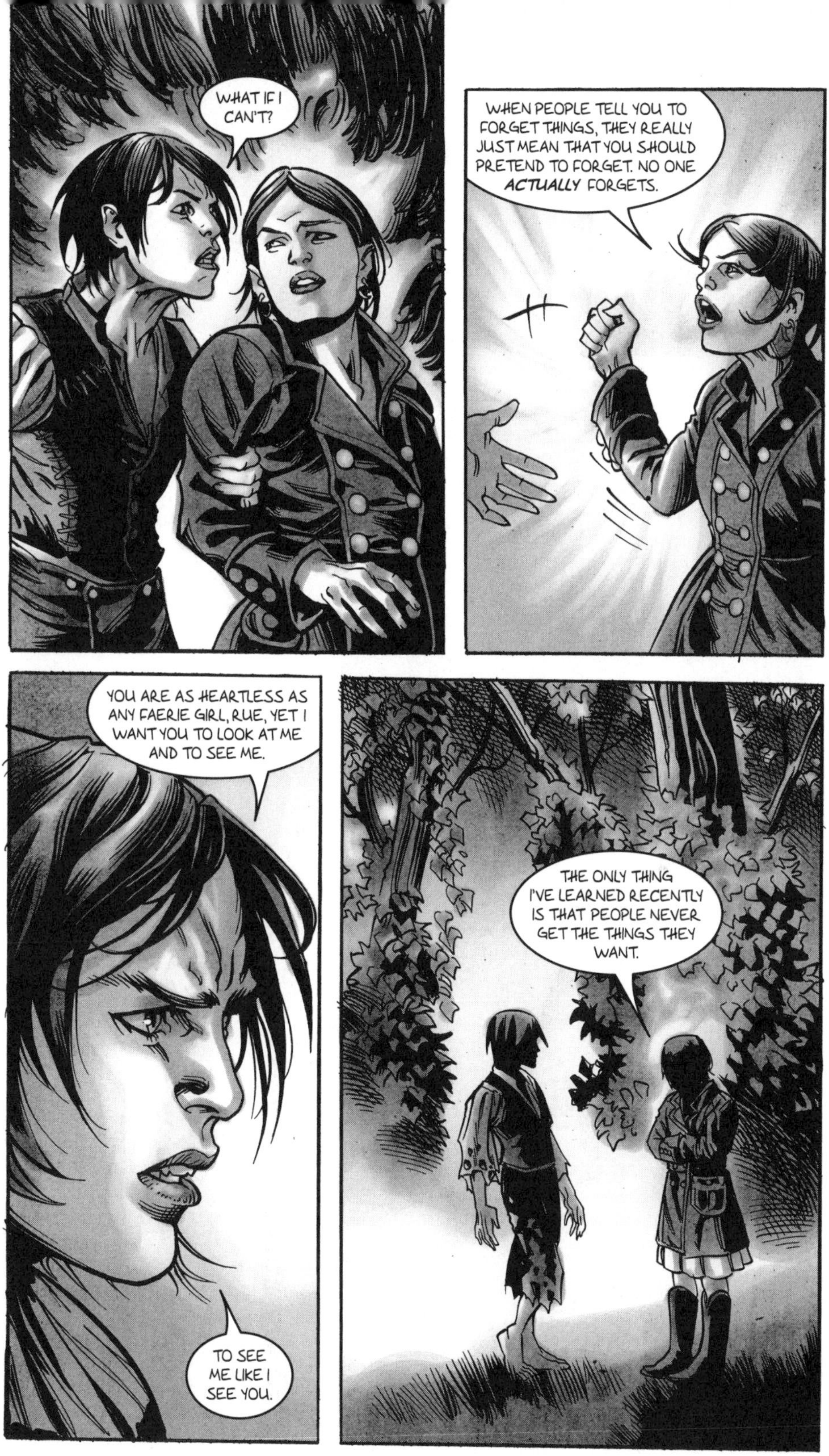
WHAT IF I CAN'T?
WHEN PEOPLE TELL YOU TO FORGET THINGS, THEY REALLY JUST MEAN THAT YOU SHOULD PRETEND TO FORGET. NO ONE *ACTUALLY* FORGETS.
YOU ARE AS HEARTLESS AS ANY FAERIE GIRL, RUE, YET I WANT YOU TO LOOK AT ME AND TO SEE ME.
TO SEE ME LIKE I SEE YOU.
THE ONLY THING I'VE LEARNED RECENTLY IS THAT PEOPLE NEVER GET THE THINGS THEY WANT.

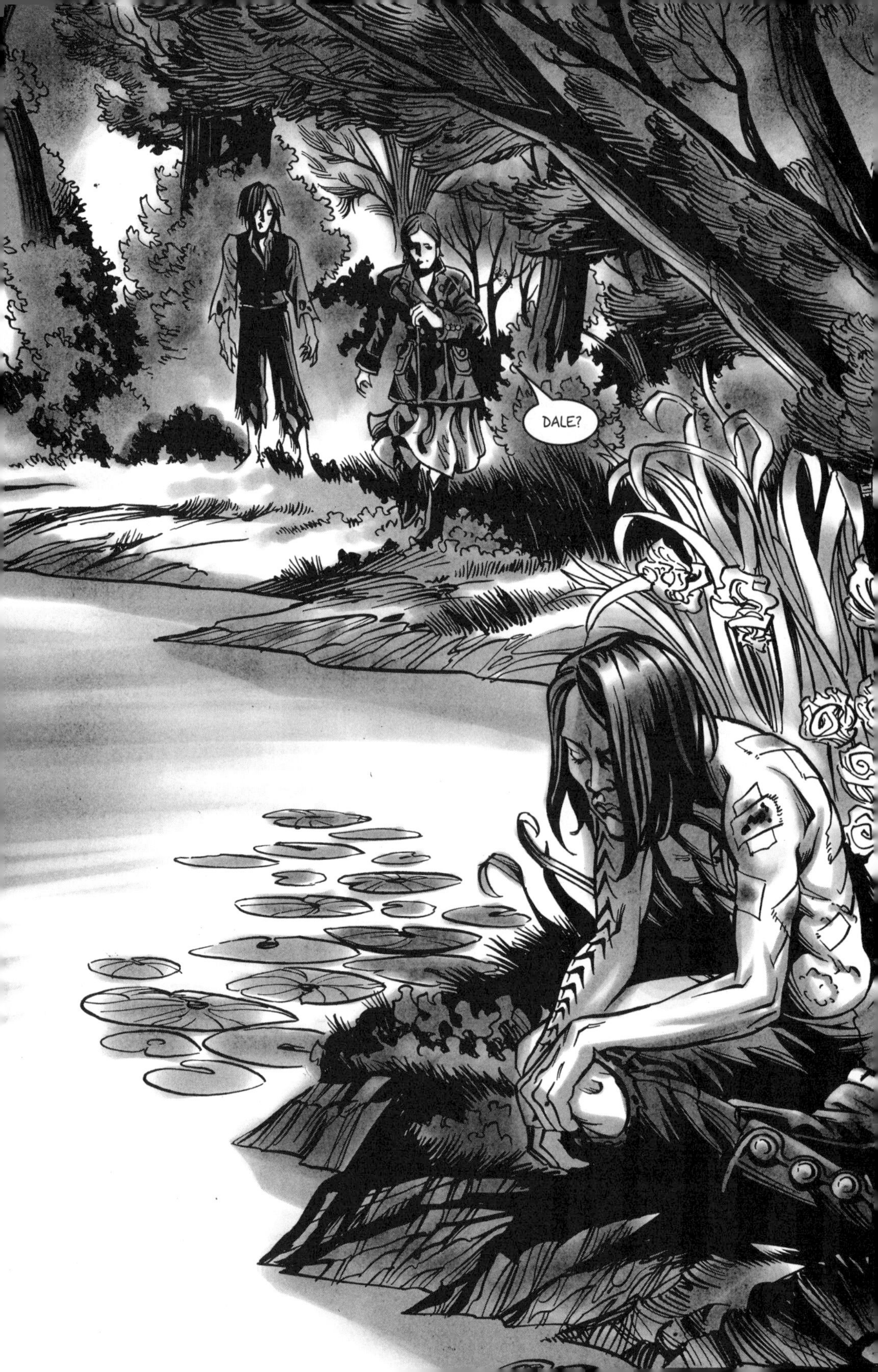
DALE?

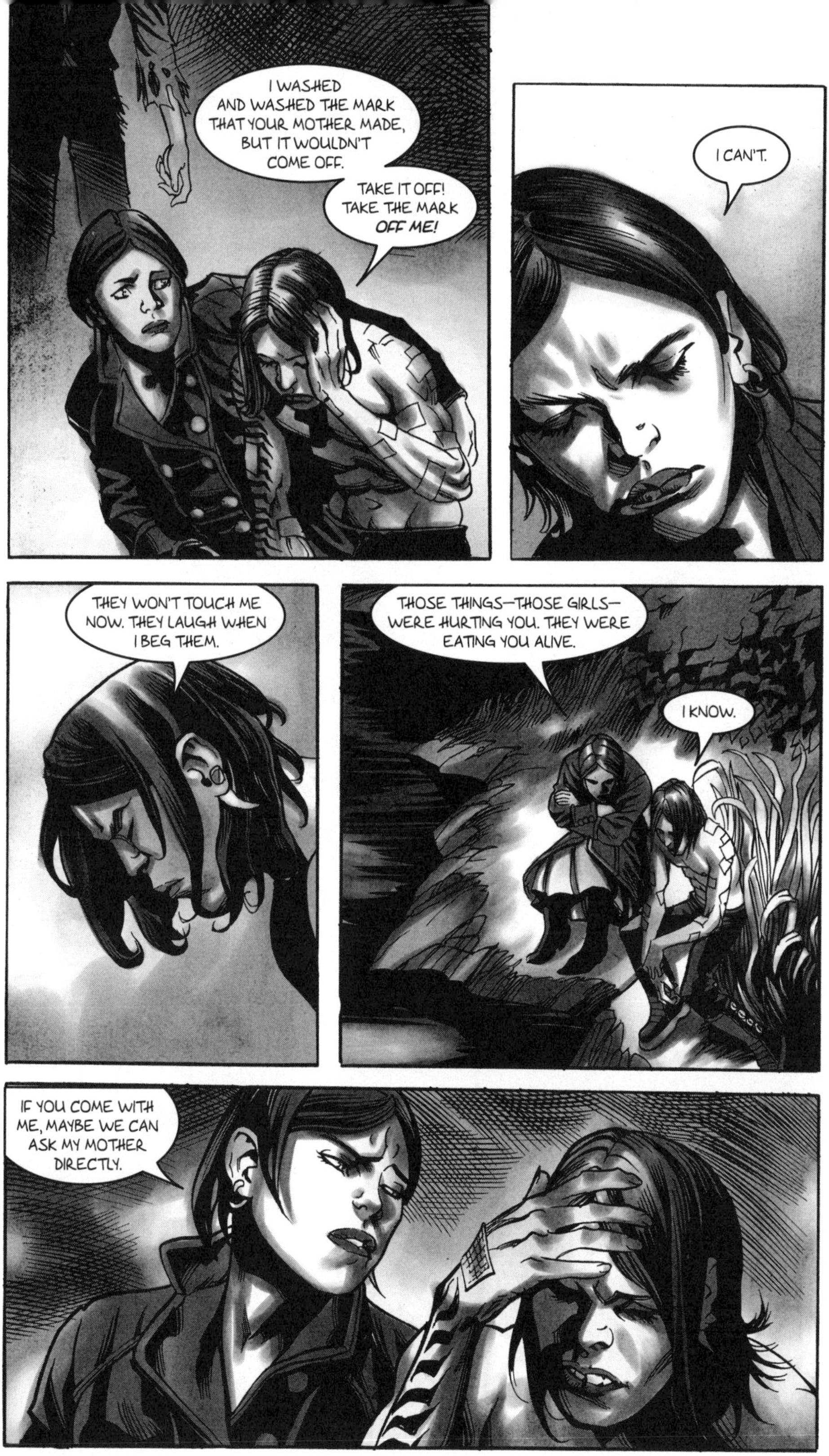
I WASHED AND WASHED THE MARK THAT YOUR MOTHER MADE, BUT IT WOULDN'T COME OFF.
TAKE IT OFF! TAKE THE MARK OFF ME!
I CAN'T.
THEY WON'T TOUCH ME NOW. THEY LAUGH WHEN I BEG THEM.
THOSE THINGS—THOSE GIRLS—WERE HURTING YOU. THEY WERE EATING YOU ALIVE.
I KNOW.
IF YOU COME WITH ME, MAYBE WE CAN ASK MY MOTHER DIRECTLY.

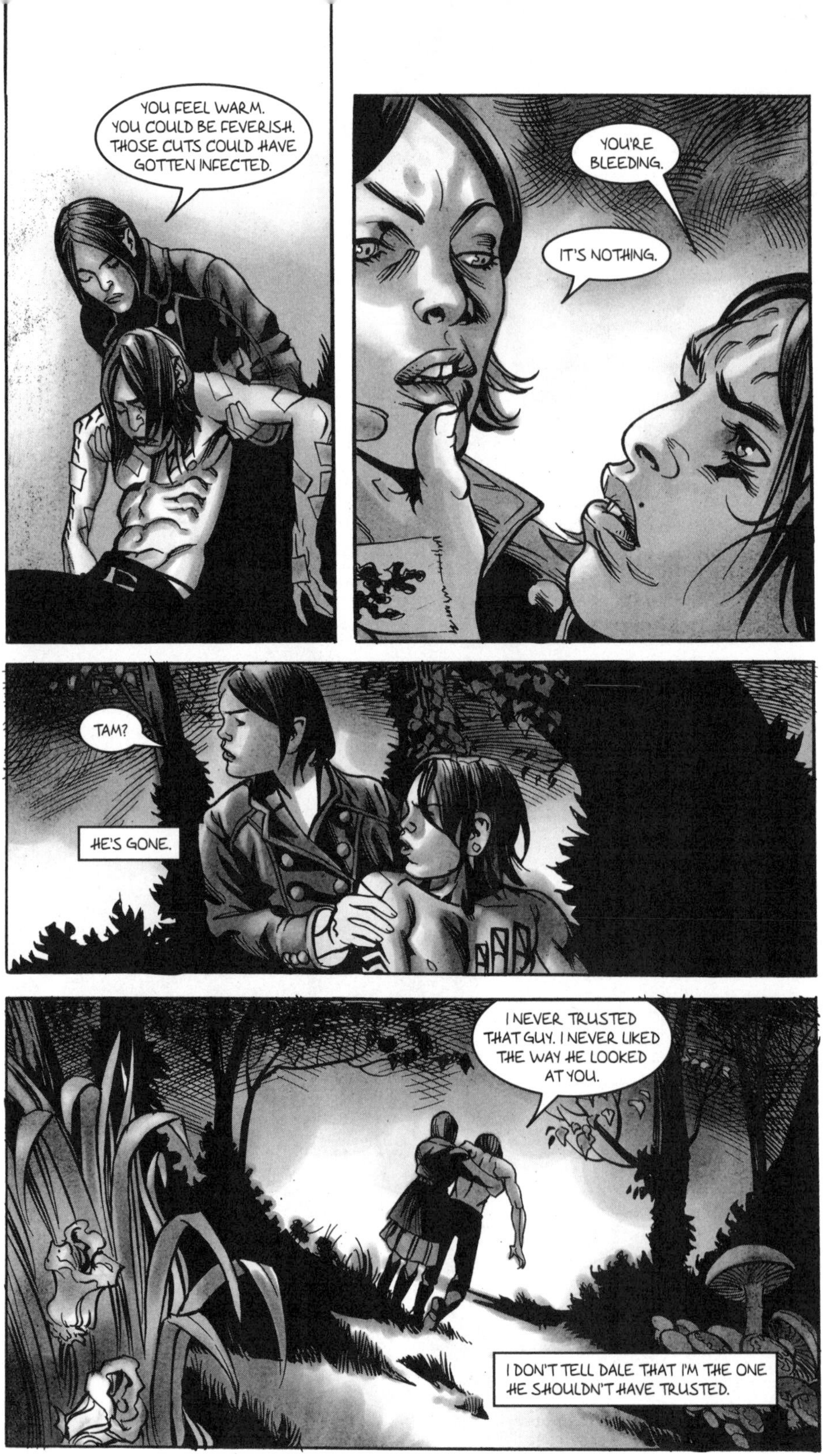
YOU FEEL WARM. YOU COULD BE FEVERISH. THOSE CUTS COULD HAVE GOTTEN INFECTED.
YOU'RE BLEEDING.
IT'S NOTHING.
TAM?
HE'S GONE.
I NEVER TRUSTED THAT GUY. I NEVER LIKED THE WAY HE LOOKED AT YOU.
I DON'T TELL DALE THAT I'M THE ONE HE SHOULDN'T HAVE TRUSTED.

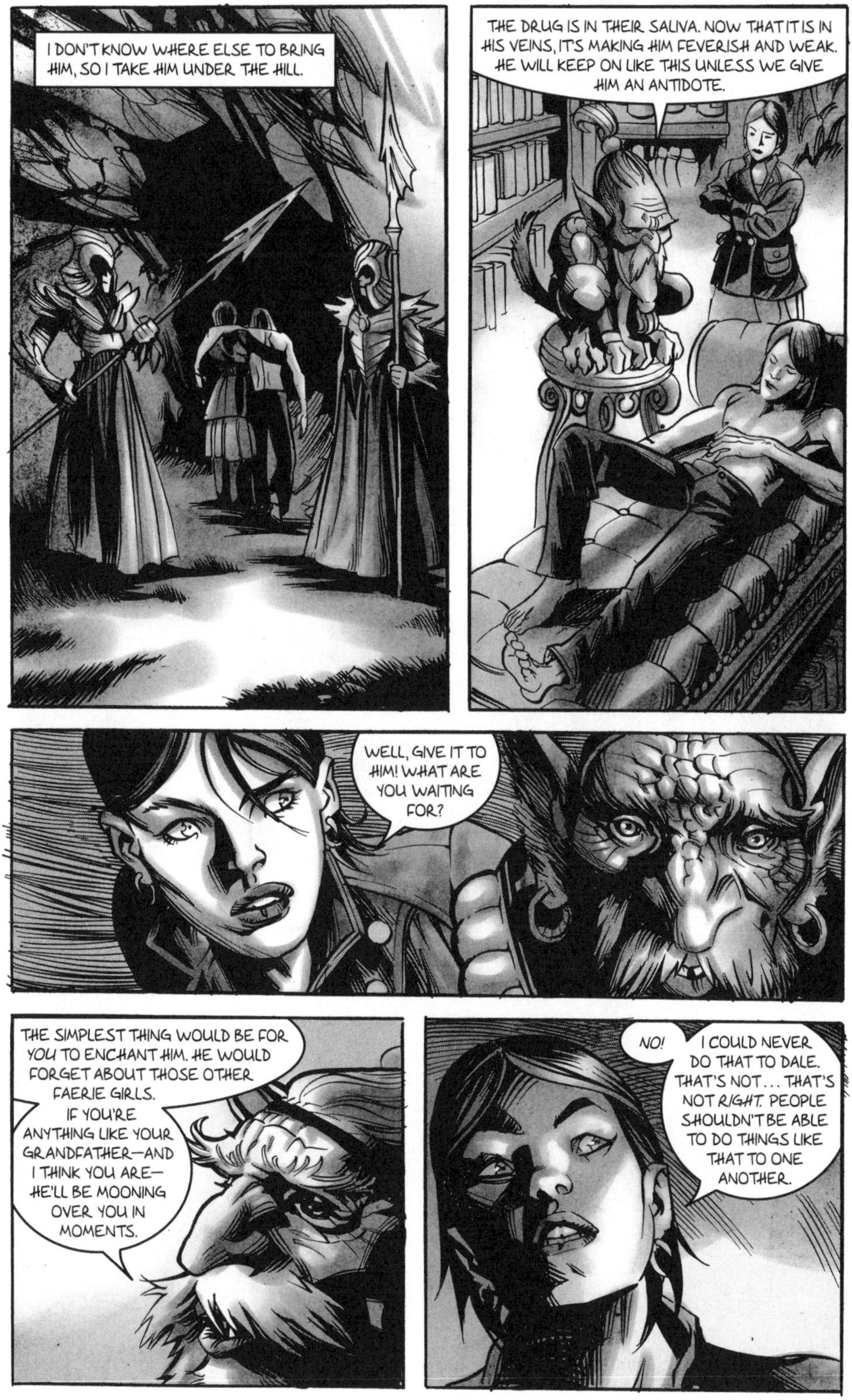
I DON'T KNOW WHERE ELSE TO BRING HIM, SO I TAKE HIM UNDER THE HILL.
THE DRUG IS IN THEIR SALIVA. NOW THAT IT IS IN HIS VEINS, IT'S MAKING HIM FEVERISH AND WEAK. HE WILL KEEP ON LIKE THIS UNLESS WE GIVE HIM AN ANTIDOTE.
WELL, GIVE IT TO HIM! WHAT ARE YOU WAITING FOR?
THE SIMPLEST THING WOULD BE FOR YOU TO ENCHANT HIM. HE WOULD FORGET ABOUT THOSE OTHER FAERIE GIRLS. IF YOU'RE ANYTHING LIKE YOUR GRANDFATHER—AND I THINK YOU ARE—HE'LL BE MOONING OVER YOU IN MOMENTS.
NO!
I COULD NEVER DO THAT TO DALE. THAT'S NOT... THAT'S NOT RIGHT. PEOPLE SHOULDN'T BE ABLE TO DO THINGS LIKE THAT TO ONE ANOTHER.

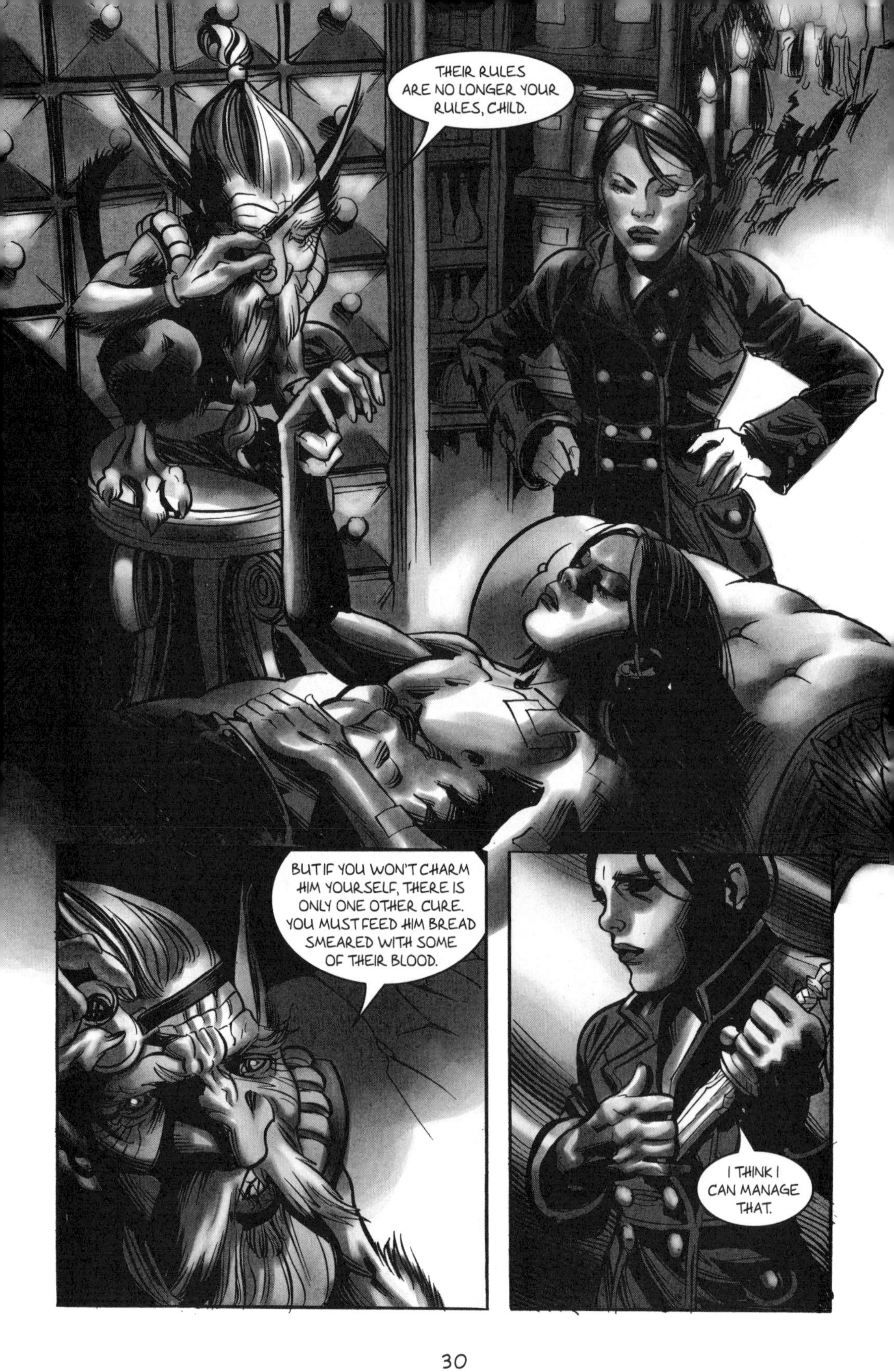
THEIR RULES ARE NO LONGER YOUR RULES, CHILD.
BUT IF YOU WON'T CHARM HIM YOURSELF, THERE IS ONLY ONE OTHER CURE. YOU MUST FEED HIM BREAD SMEARED WITH SOME OF THEIR BLOOD.
I THINK I CAN MANAGE THAT.

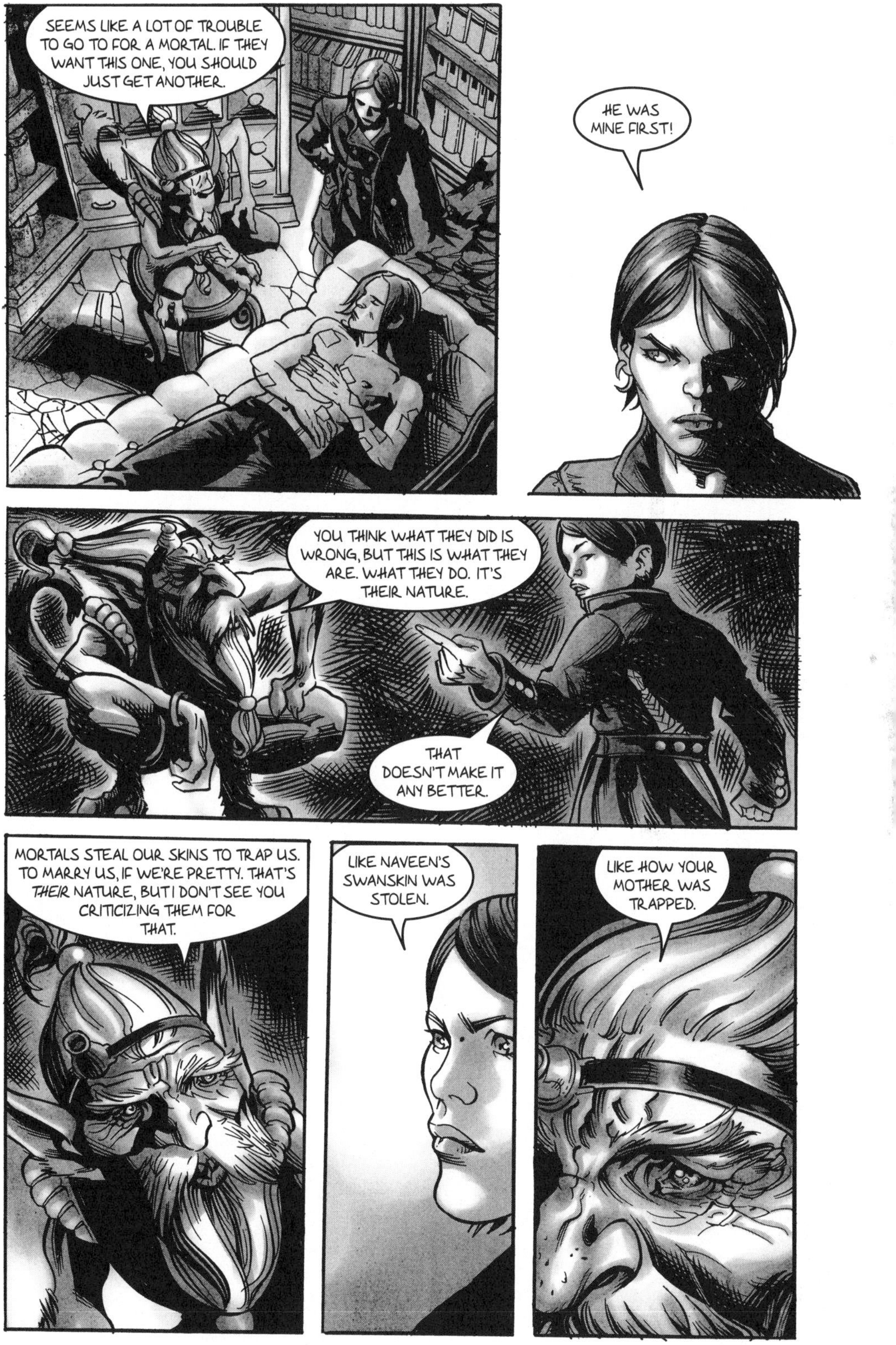
SEEMS LIKE A LOT OF TROUBLE TO GO TO FOR A MORTAL. IF THEY WANT THIS ONE, YOU SHOULD JUST GET ANOTHER.
HE WAS MINE FIRST!
YOU THINK WHAT THEY DID IS WRONG, BUT THIS IS WHAT THEY ARE. WHAT THEY DO. IT'S THEIR NATURE.
THAT DOESN'T MAKE IT ANY BETTER.
MORTALS STEAL OUR SKINS TO TRAP US. TO MARRY US, IF WE'RE PRETTY. THAT'S *THEIR* NATURE, BUT I DON'T SEE YOU CRITICIZING THEM FOR THAT.
LIKE NAVEEN'S SWANSKIN WAS STOLEN.
LIKE HOW YOUR MOTHER WAS TRAPPED.

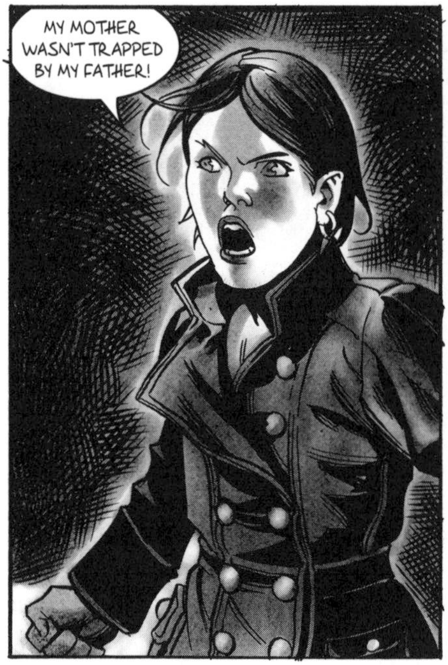
MY MOTHER WASN'T TRAPPED BY MY FATHER!

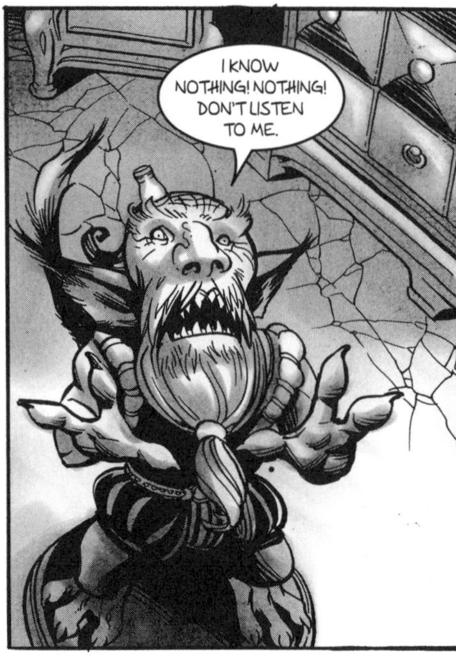
I KNOW NOTHING! NOTHING! DON'T LISTEN TO ME.

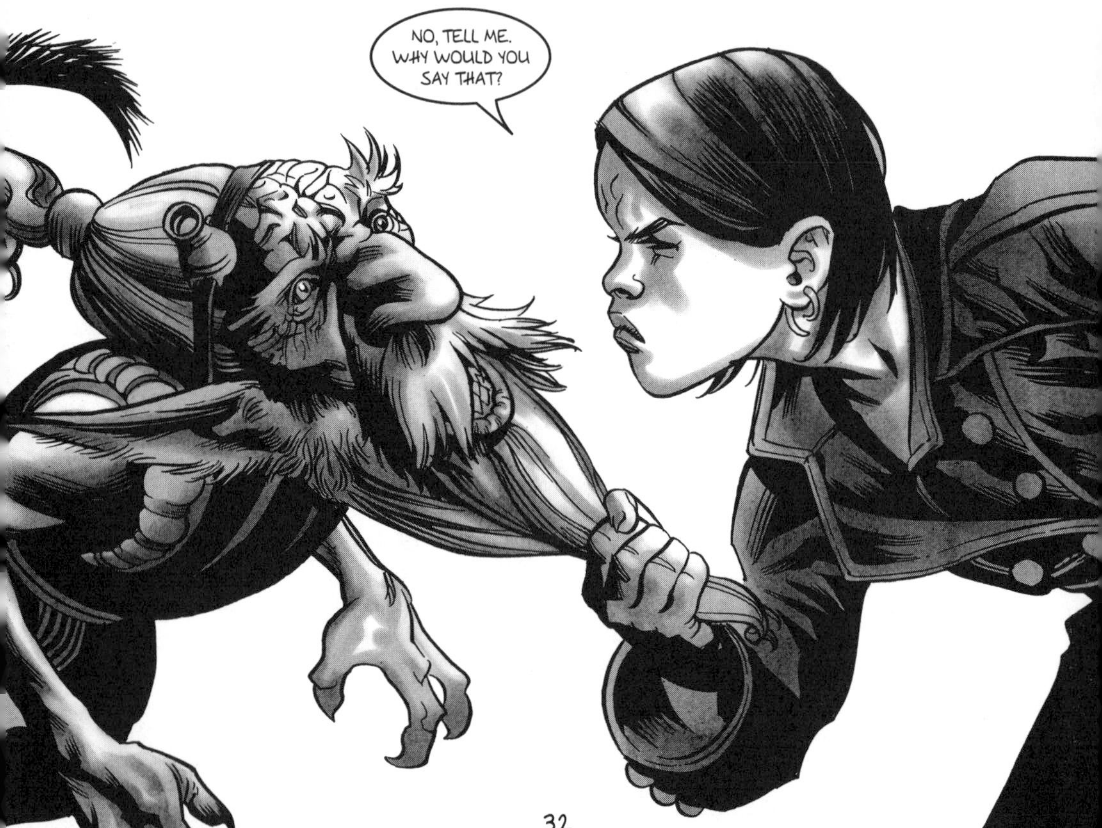
NO, TELL ME. WHY WOULD YOU SAY THAT?

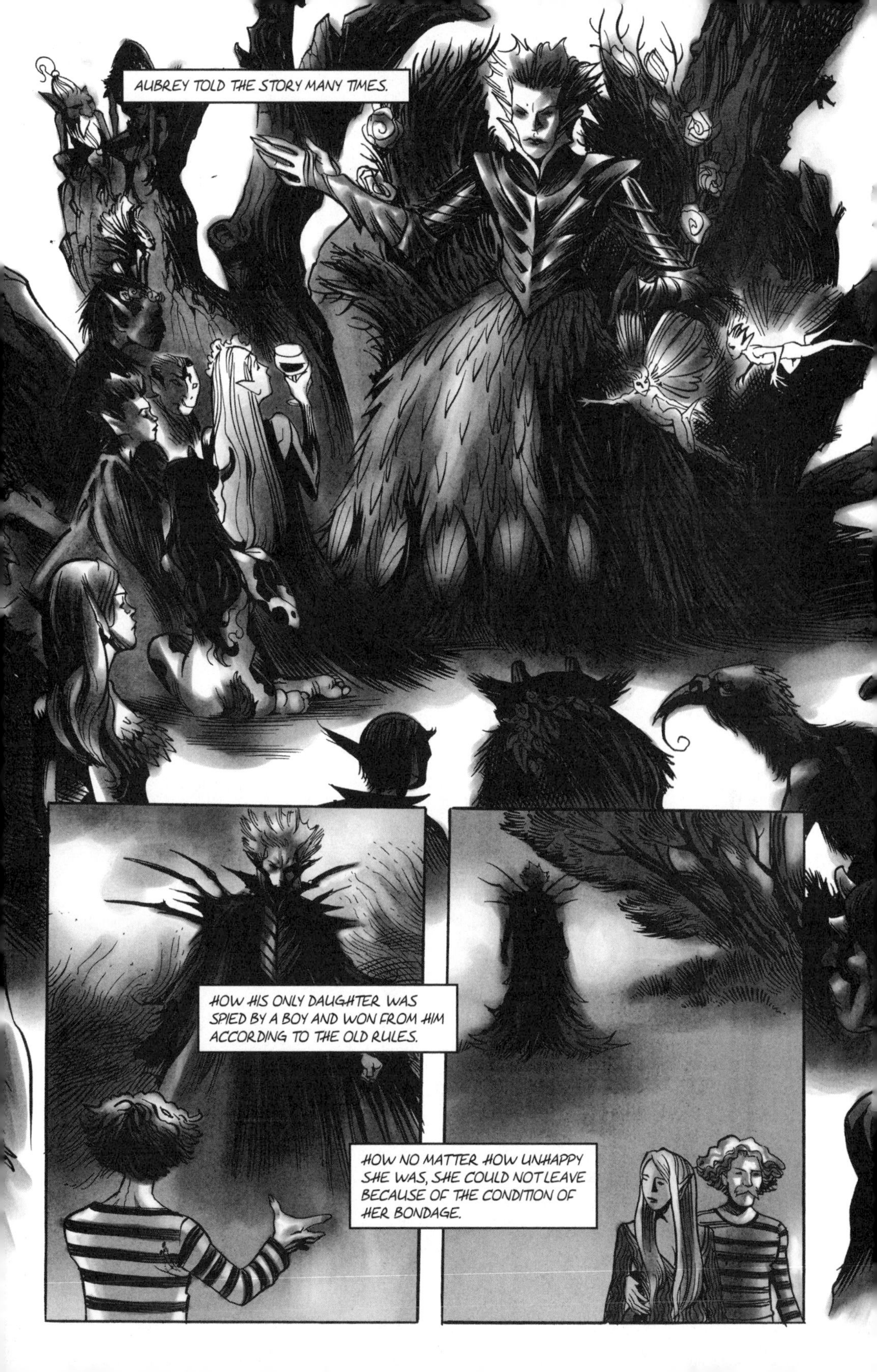
AUBREY TOLD THE STORY MANY TIMES.
HOW HIS ONLY DAUGHTER WAS SPIED BY A BOY AND WON FROM HIM ACCORDING TO THE OLD RULES.
HOW NO MATTER HOW UNHAPPY SHE WAS, SHE COULD NOT LEAVE BECAUSE OF THE CONDITION OF HER BONDAGE.

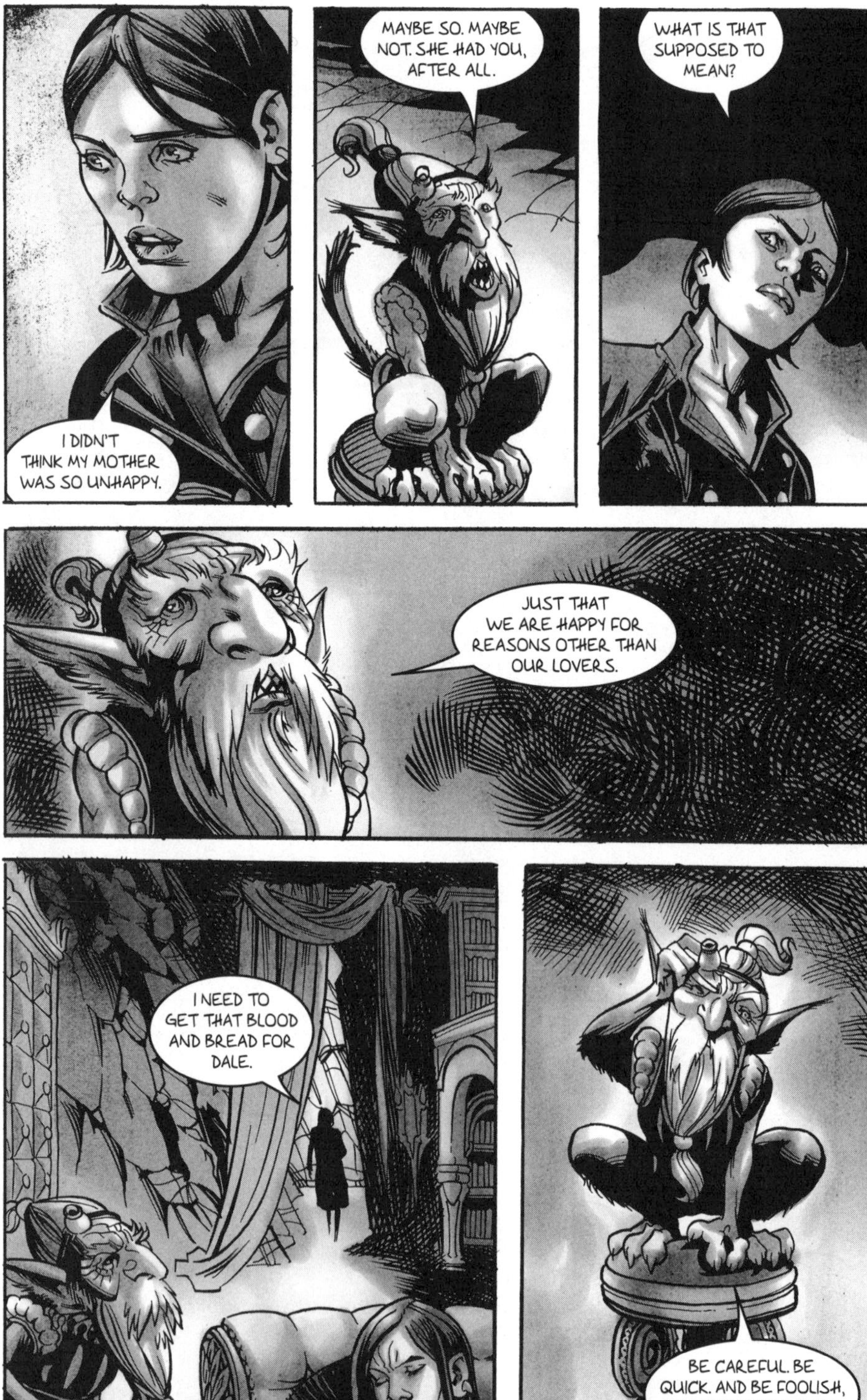
I DIDN'T THINK MY MOTHER WAS SO UNHAPPY.
MAYBE SO. MAYBE NOT. SHE HAD YOU, AFTER ALL.
WHAT IS THAT SUPPOSED TO MEAN?
JUST THAT WE ARE HAPPY FOR REASONS OTHER THAN OUR LOVERS.
I NEED TO GET THAT BLOOD AND BREAD FOR DALE.
BE CAREFUL. BE QUICK. AND BE FOOLISH, BECAUSE FATE LOVES A FOOL.

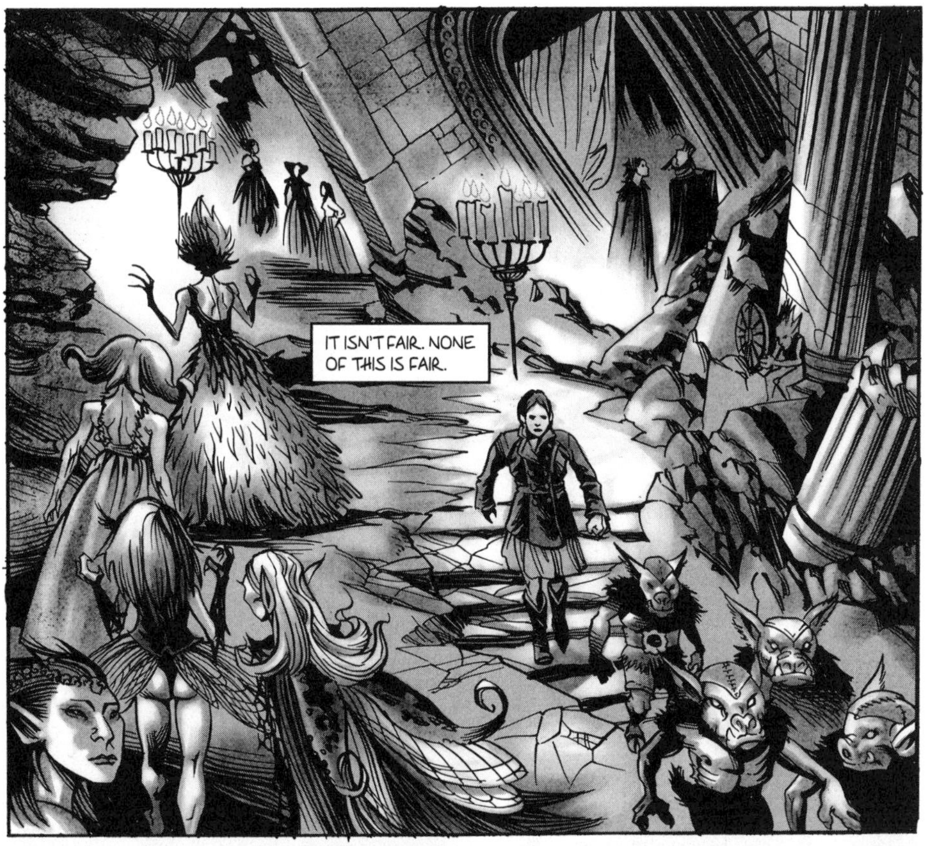
IT ISN'T FAIR. NONE OF THIS IS FAIR.

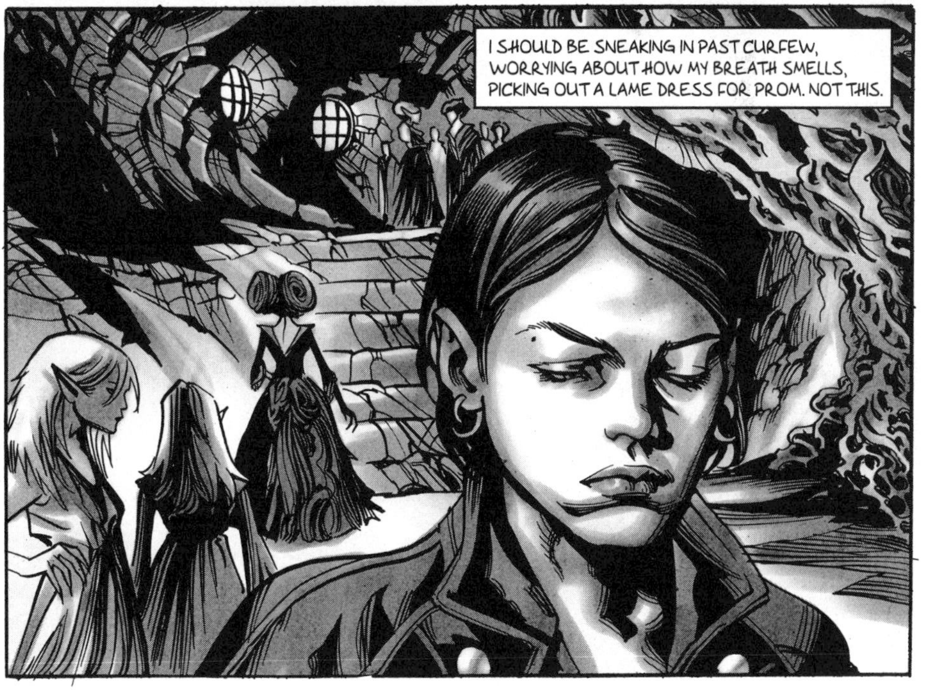
I SHOULD BE SNEAKING IN PAST CURFEW, WORRYING ABOUT HOW MY BREATH SMELLS, PICKING OUT A LAME DRESS FOR PROM. NOT THIS.

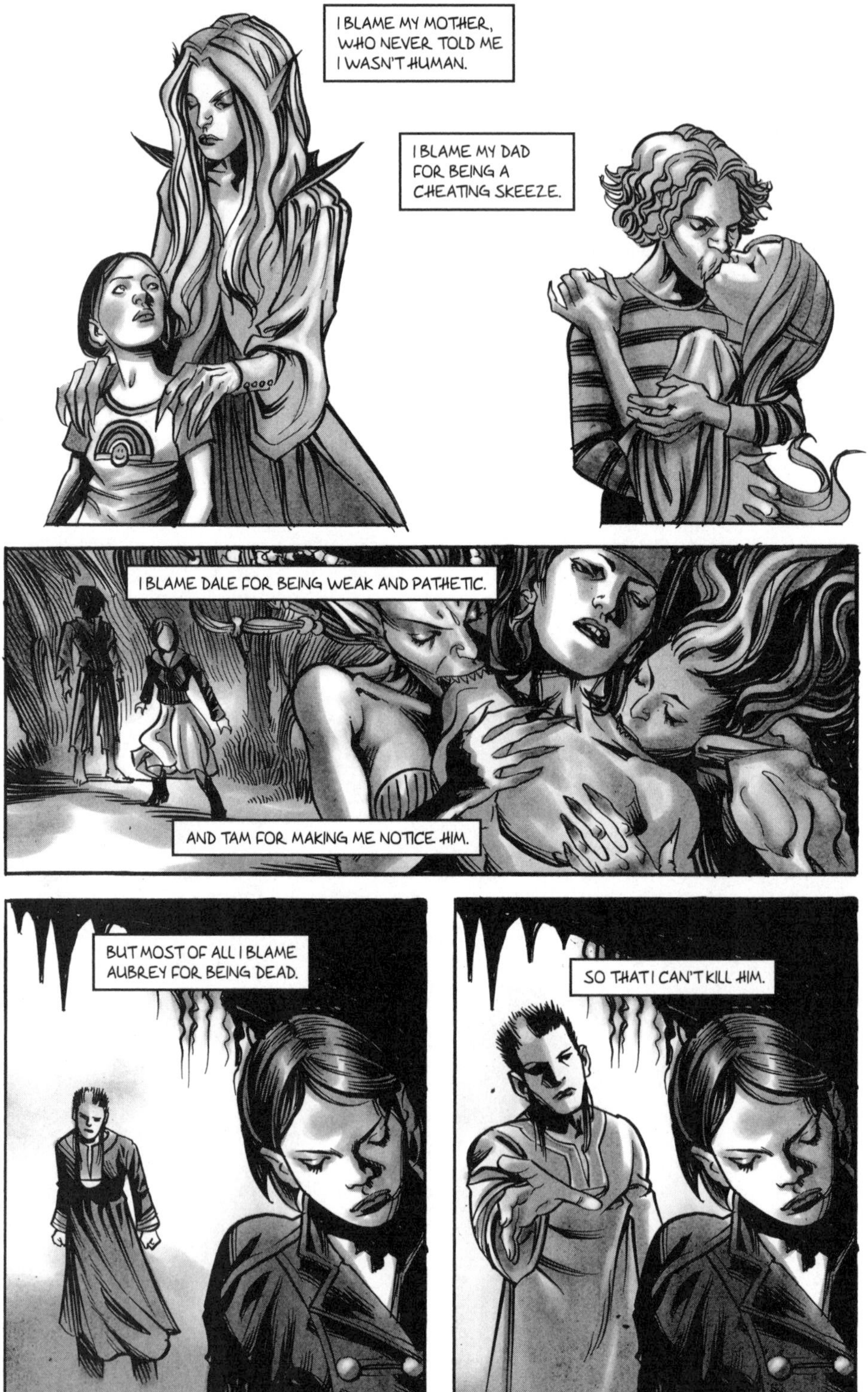
I BLAME MY MOTHER, WHO NEVER TOLD ME I WASN'T HUMAN.
I BLAME MY DAD FOR BEING A CHEATING SKEEZE.
I BLAME DALE FOR BEING WEAK AND PATHETIC.
AND TAM FOR MAKING ME NOTICE HIM.
BUT MOST OF ALL I BLAME AUBREY FOR BEING DEAD.
SO THAT I CAN'T KILL HIM.

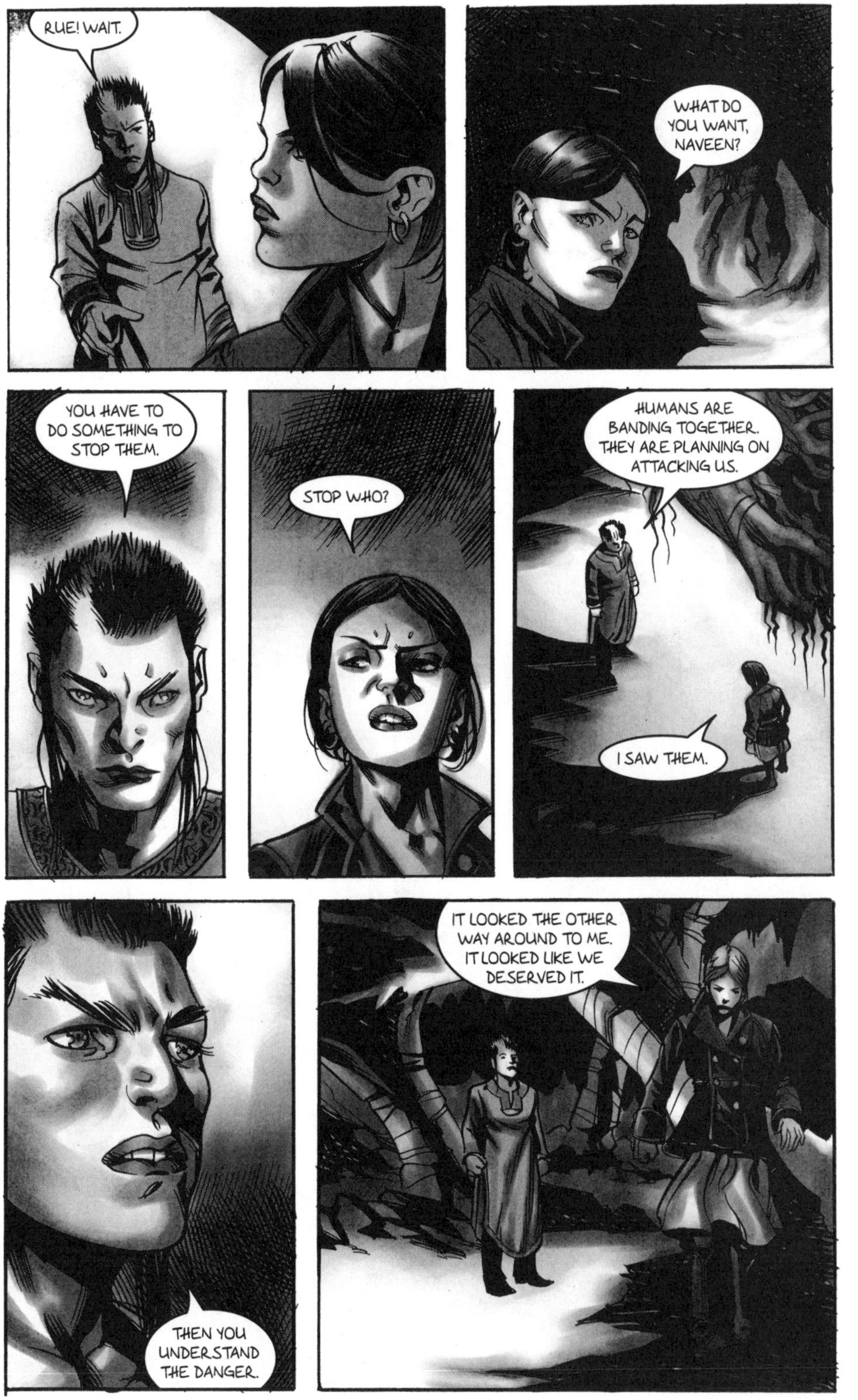
RUE! WAIT.
WHAT DO YOU WANT, NAVEEN?
YOU HAVE TO DO SOMETHING TO STOP THEM.
STOP WHO?
HUMANS ARE BANDING TOGETHER. THEY ARE PLANNING ON ATTACKING US.
I SAW THEM.
THEN YOU UNDERSTAND THE DANGER.
IT LOOKED THE OTHER WAY AROUND TO ME. IT LOOKED LIKE WE DESERVED IT.

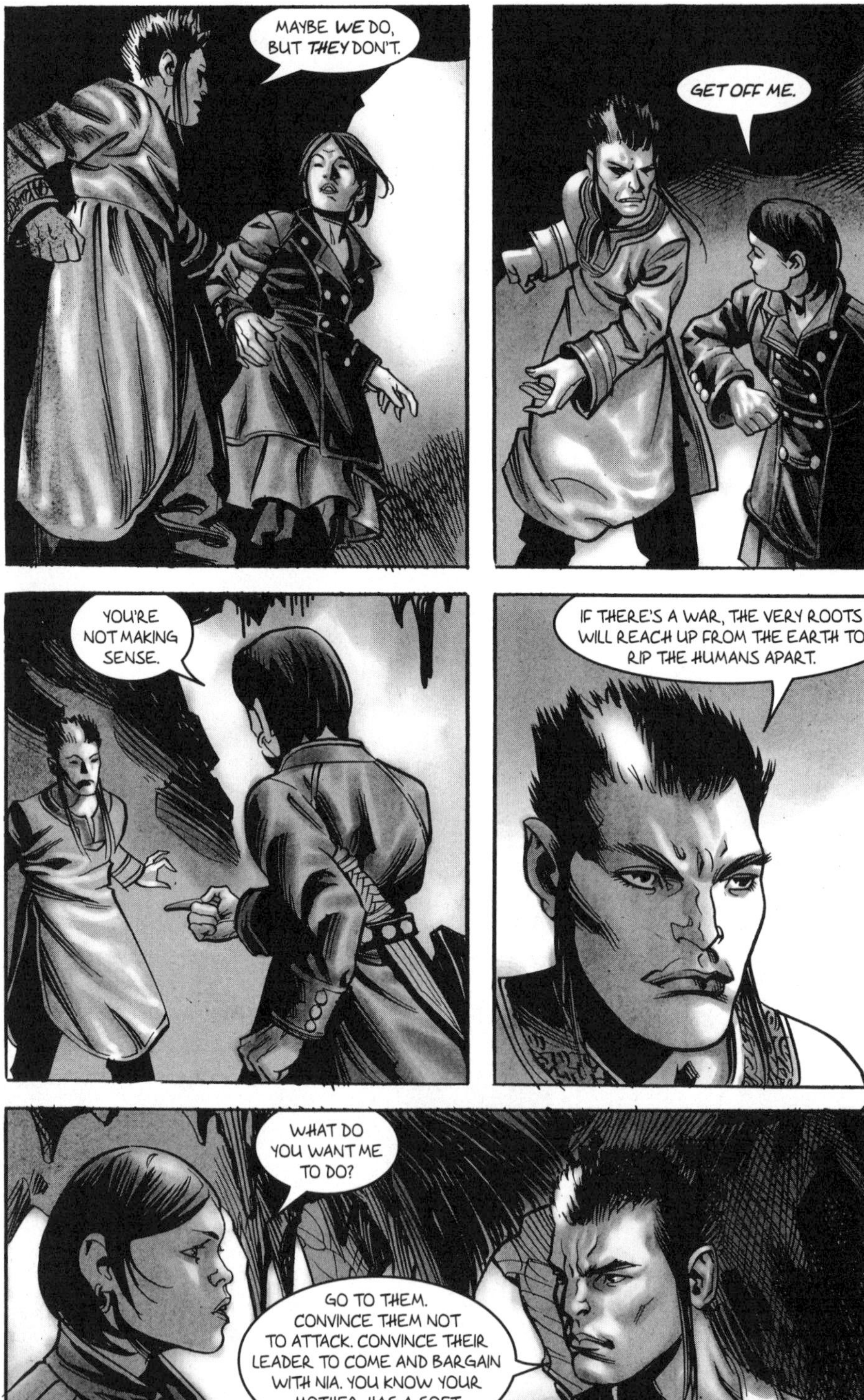
MAYBE WE DO, BUT THEY DON'T.
GET OFF ME.
YOU'RE NOT MAKING SENSE.
IF THERE'S A WAR, THE VERY ROOTS WILL REACH UP FROM THE EARTH TO RIP THE HUMANS APART.
WHAT DO YOU WANT ME TO DO?
GO TO THEM. CONVINCE THEM NOT TO ATTACK. CONVINCE THEIR LEADER TO COME AND BARGAIN WITH NIA. YOU KNOW YOUR MOTHER HAS A SOFT HEART.

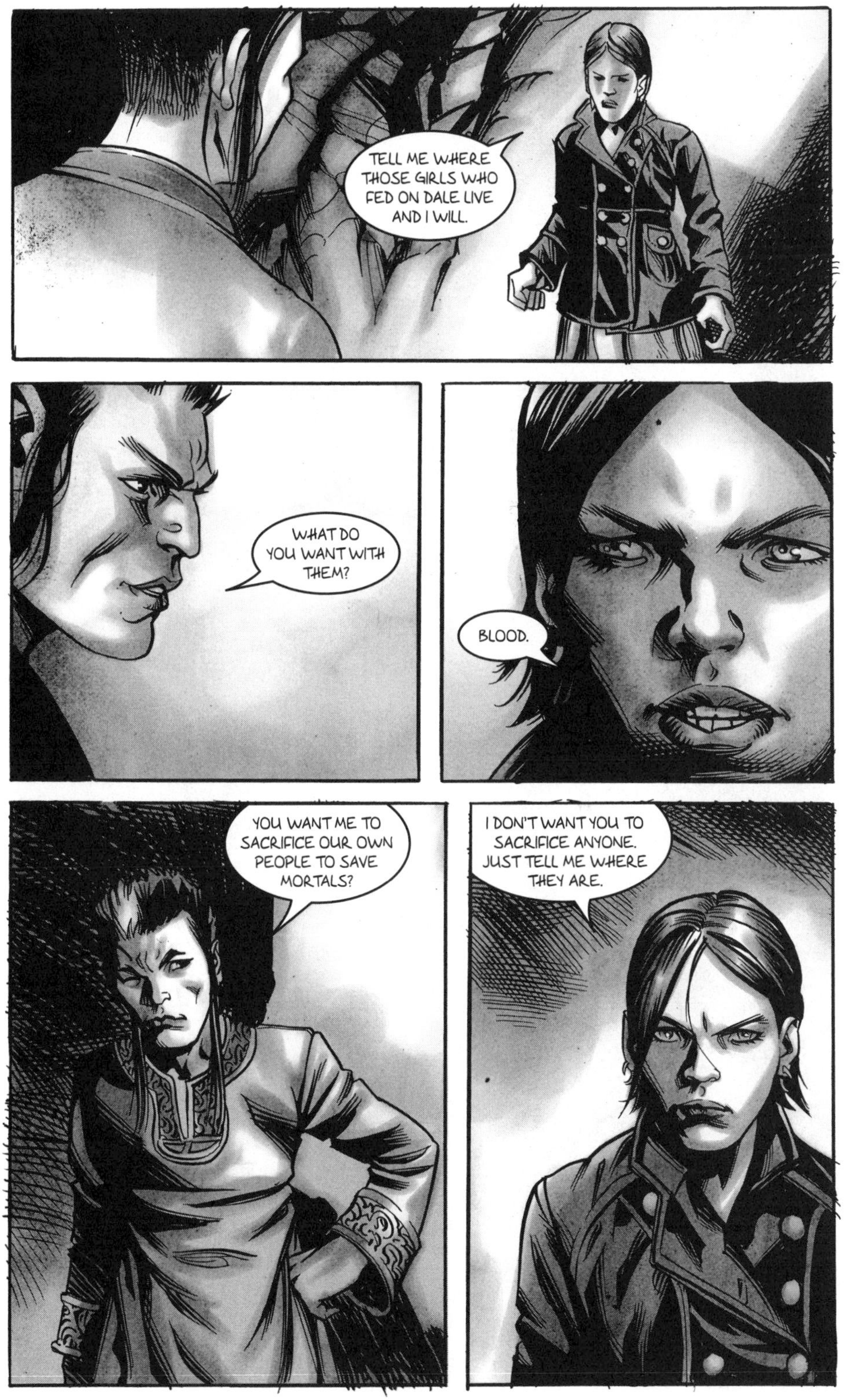
TELL ME WHERE THOSE GIRLS WHO FED ON DALE LIVE AND I WILL.
WHAT DO YOU WANT WITH THEM?
BLOOD.
YOU WANT ME TO SACRIFICE OUR OWN PEOPLE TO SAVE MORTALS?
I DON'T WANT YOU TO SACRIFICE ANYONE. JUST TELL ME WHERE THEY ARE.

40

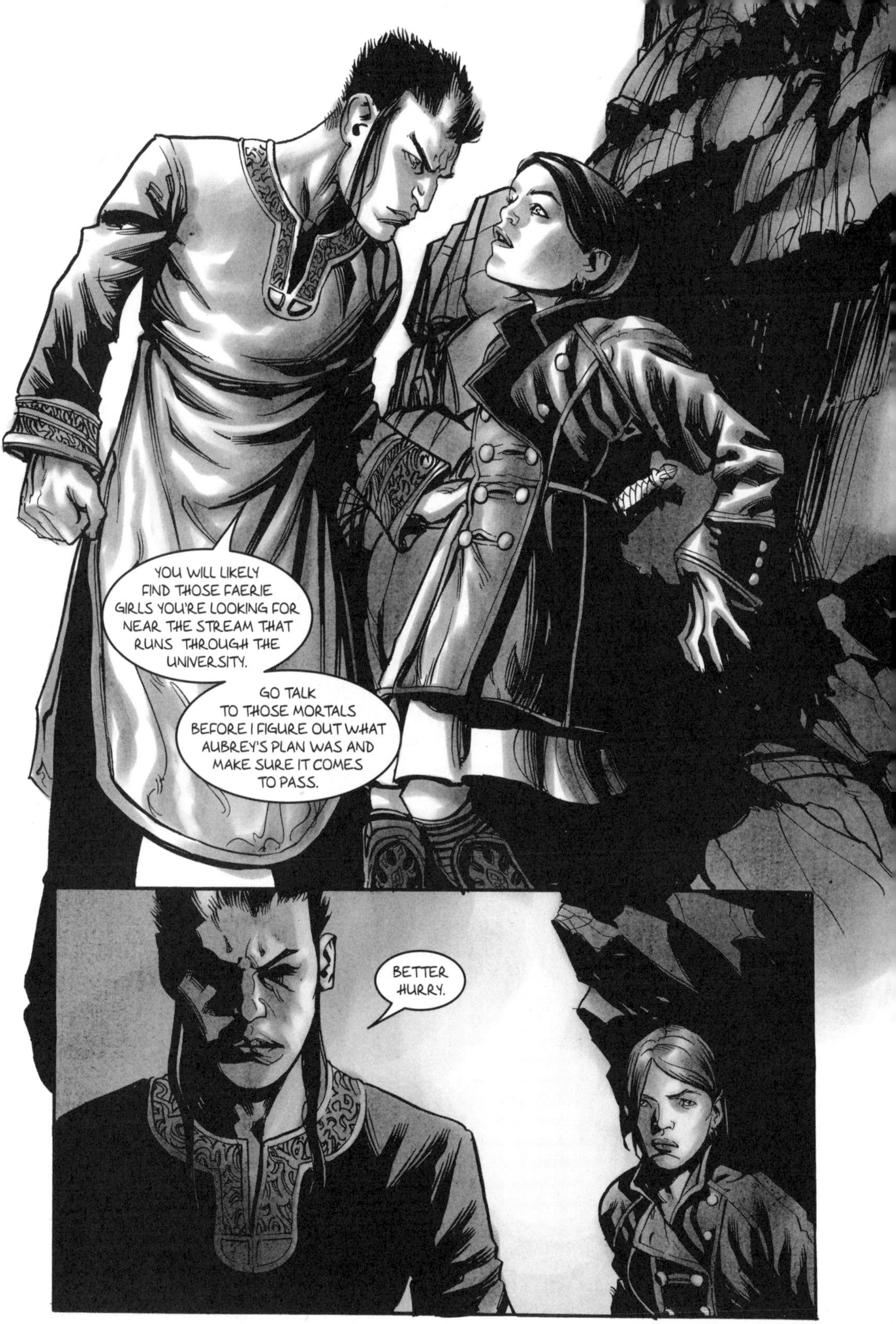
YOU WILL LIKELY FIND THOSE FAERIE GIRLS YOU'RE LOOKING FOR NEAR THE STREAM THAT RUNS THROUGH THE UNIVERSITY.
GO TALK TO THOSE MORTALS BEFORE I FIGURE OUT WHAT AUBREY'S PLAN WAS AND MAKE SURE IT COMES TO PASS.
BETTER HURRY.

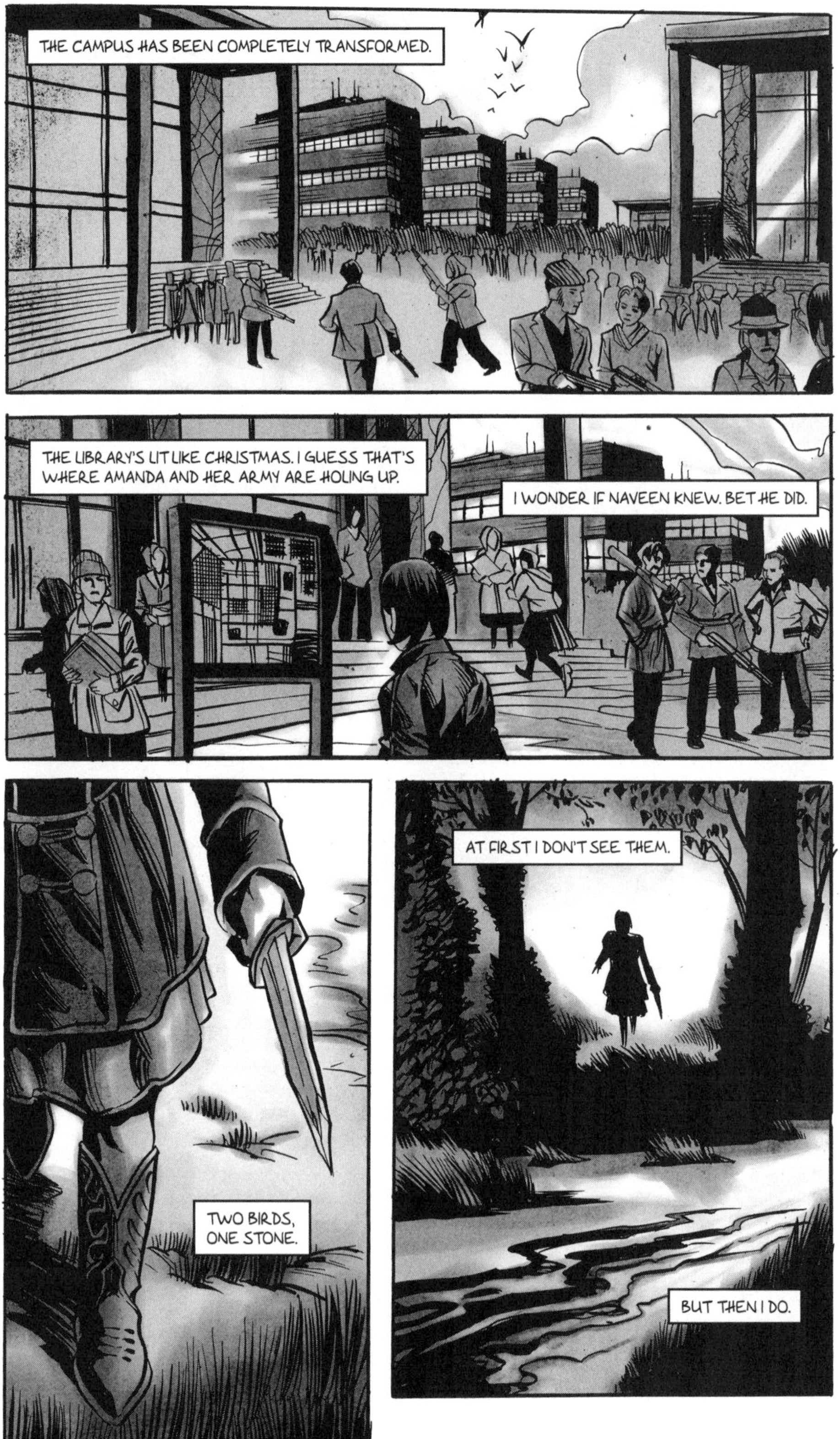
THE CAMPUS HAS BEEN COMPLETELY TRANSFORMED.
THE LIBRARY'S LIT LIKE CHRISTMAS. I GUESS THAT'S WHERE AMANDA AND HER ARMY ARE HOLING UP.
I WONDER IF NAVEEN KNEW. BET HE DID.
TWO BIRDS, ONE STONE.
AT FIRST I DON'T SEE THEM.
BUT THEN I DO.

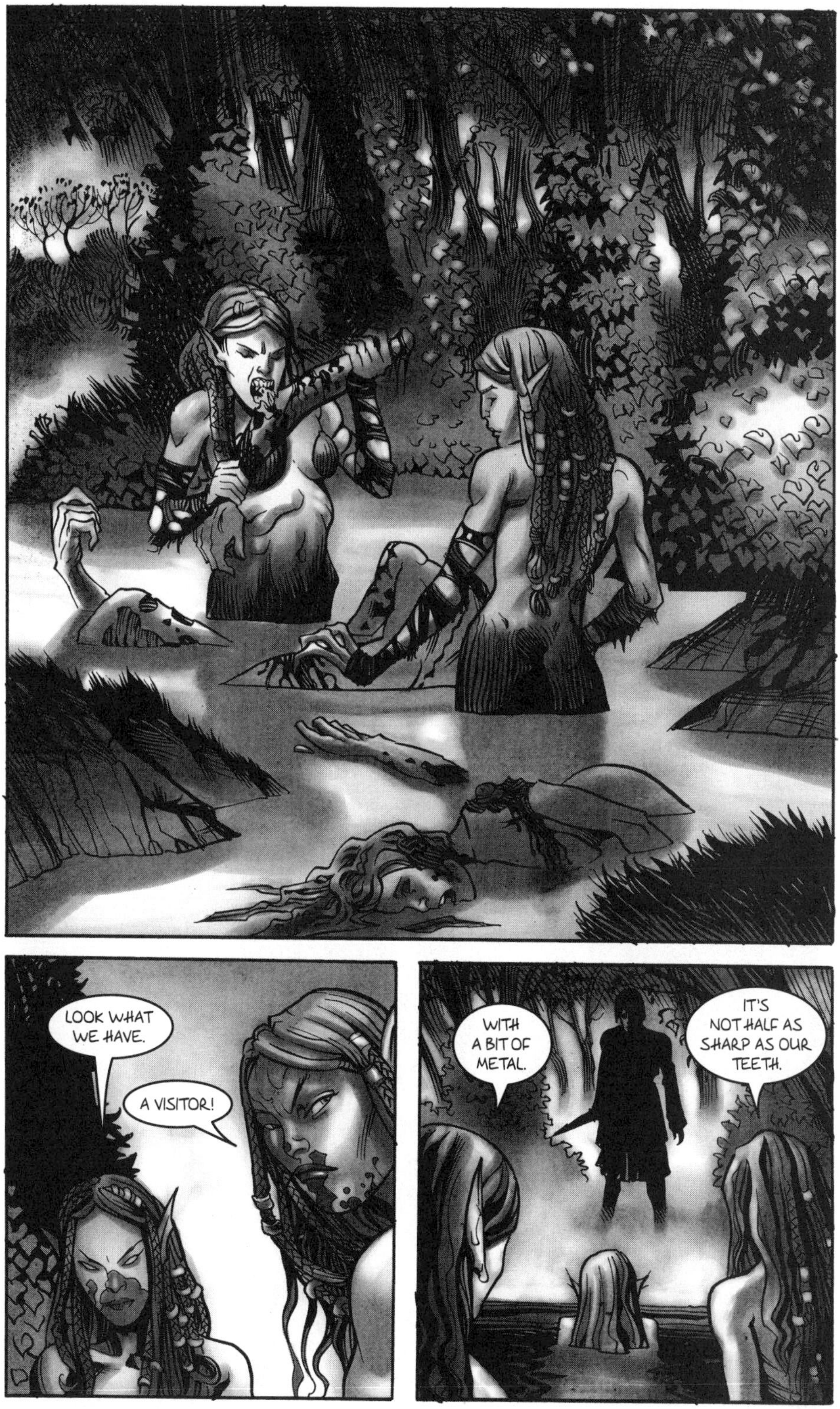
LOOK WHAT WE HAVE.
A VISITOR!
WITH A BIT OF METAL.
IT'S NOT HALF AS SHARP AS OUR TEETH.

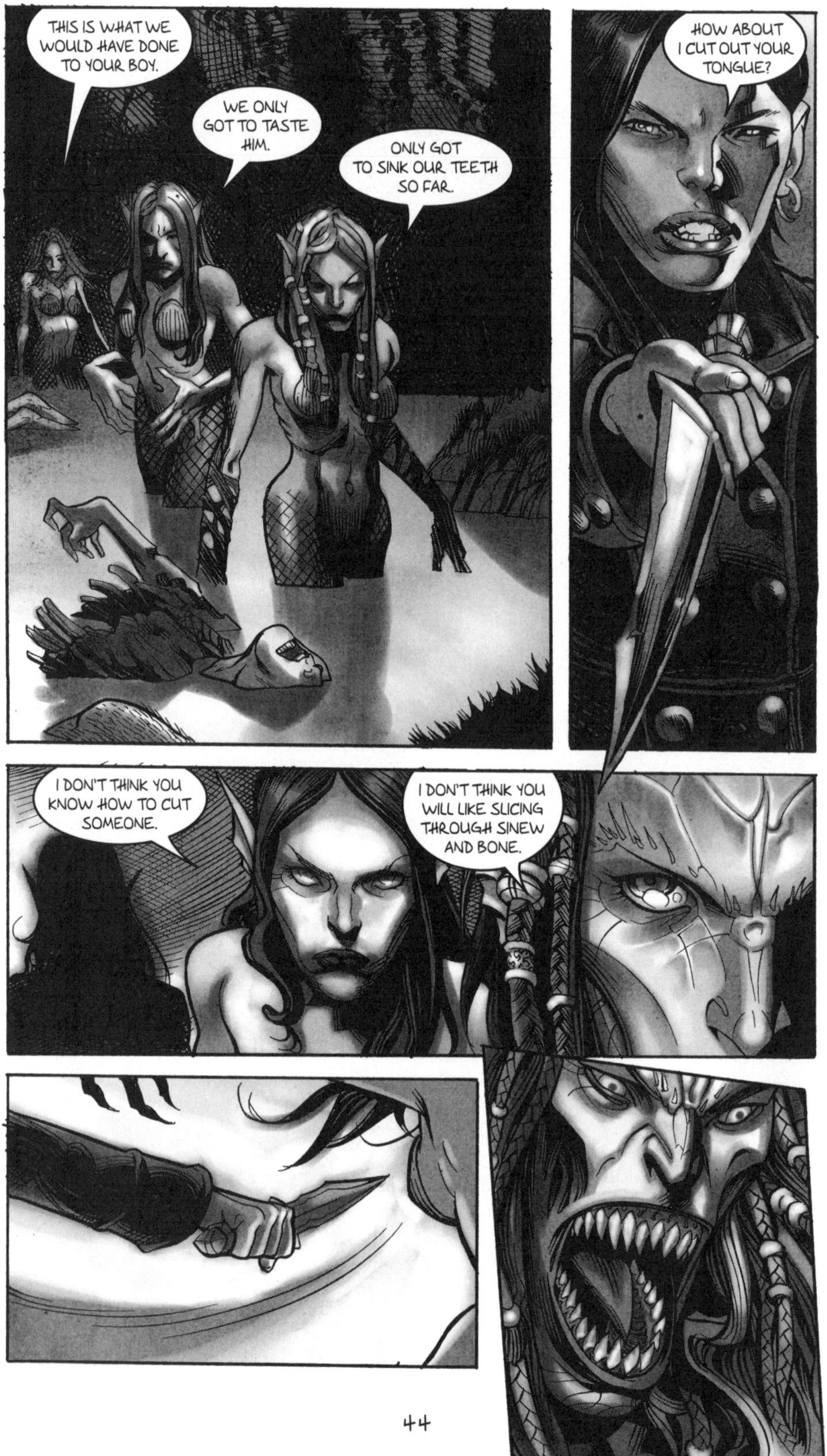

THIS IS WHAT WE WOULD HAVE DONE TO YOUR BOY.
WE ONLY GOT TO TASTE HIM.
ONLY GOT TO SINK OUR TEETH SO FAR.
HOW ABOUT I CUT OUT YOUR TONGUE?
I DON'T THINK YOU KNOW HOW TO CUT SOMEONE.
I DON'T THINK YOU WILL LIKE SLICING THROUGH SINEW AND BONE.

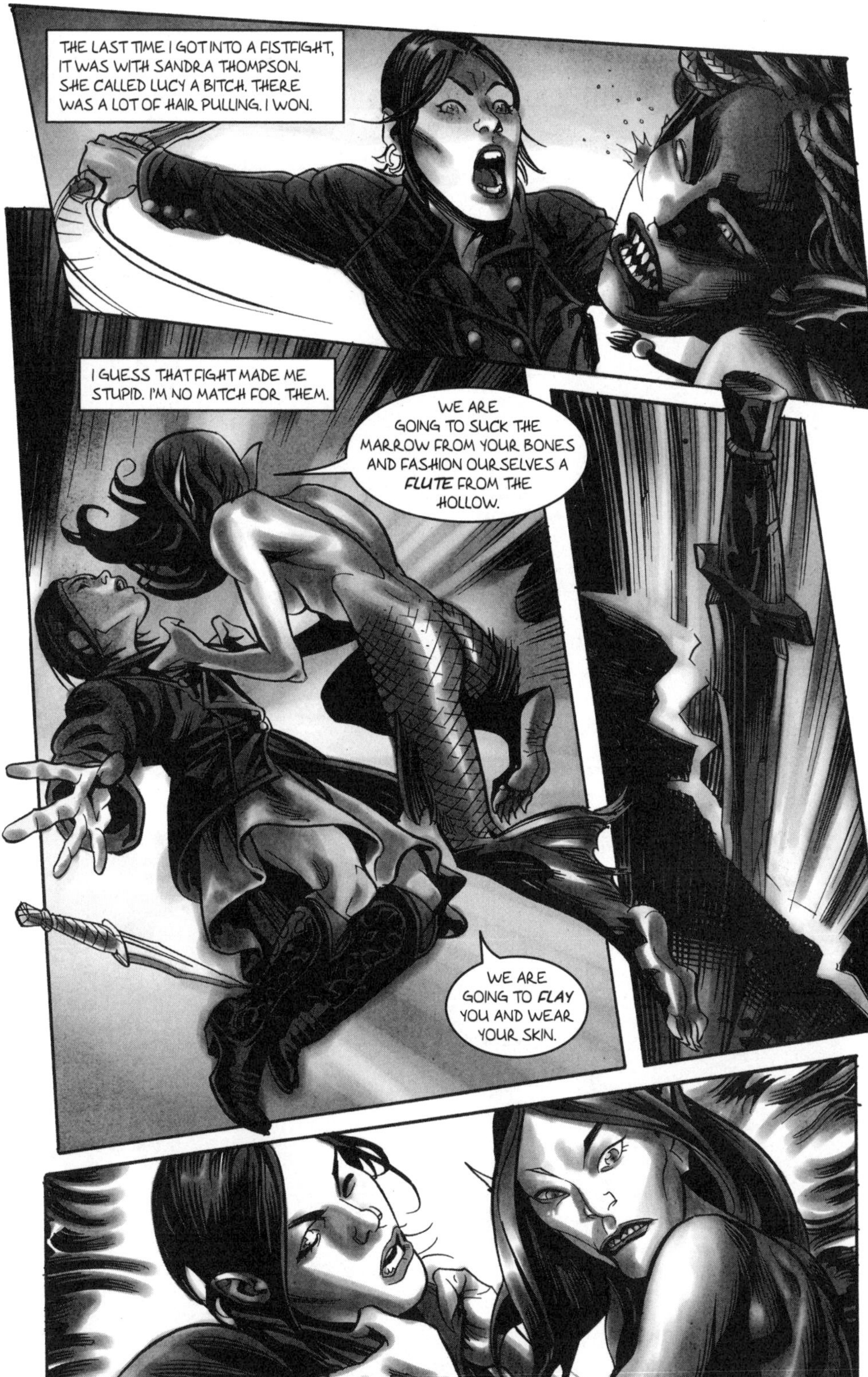
THE LAST TIME I GOT INTO A FISTFIGHT, IT WAS WITH SANDRA THOMPSON. SHE CALLED LUCY A BITCH. THERE WAS A LOT OF HAIR PULLING. I WON.
I GUESS THAT FIGHT MADE ME STUPID. I'M NO MATCH FOR THEM.
WE ARE GOING TO SUCK THE MARROW FROM YOUR BONES AND FASHION OURSELVES A *FLUTE* FROM THE HOLLOW.
WE ARE GOING TO *FLAY* YOU AND WEAR YOUR SKIN.

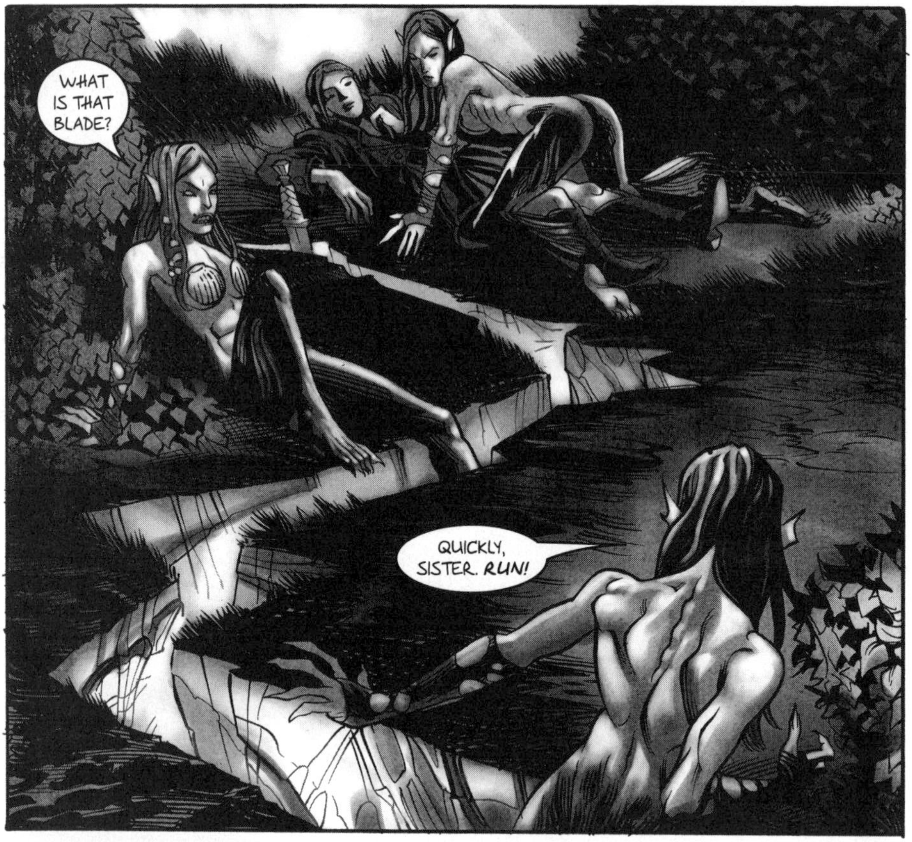
WHAT IS THAT BLADE?
QUICKLY, SISTER. RUN!

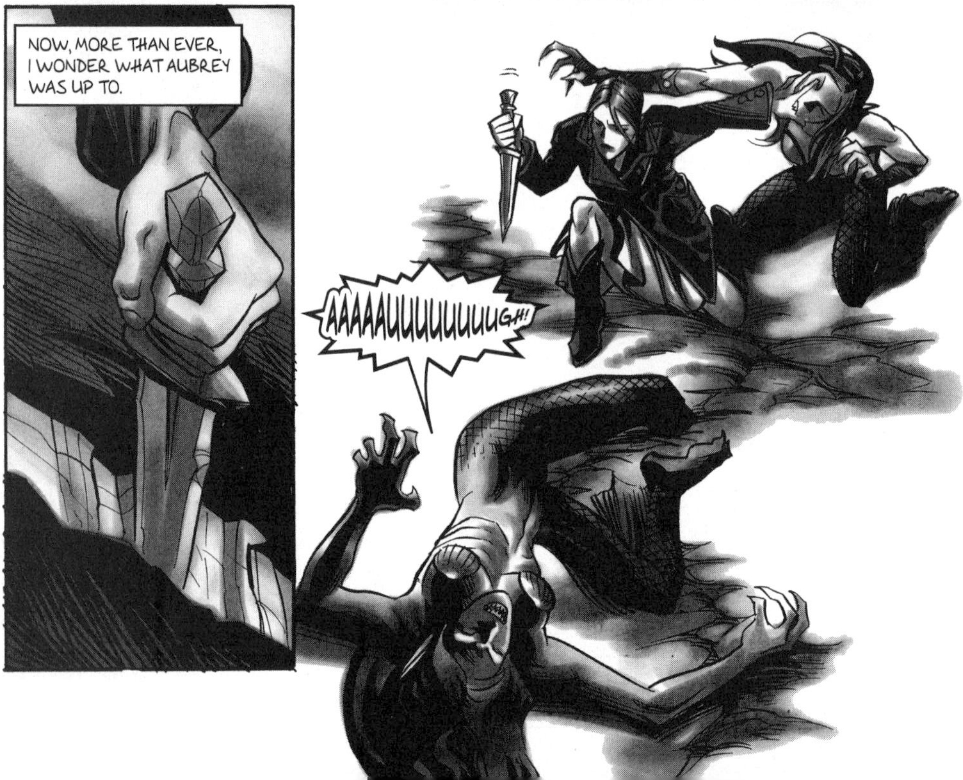
NOW, MORE THAN EVER, I WONDER WHAT AUBREY WAS UP TO.
AAAAAUUUUUUUUGH!

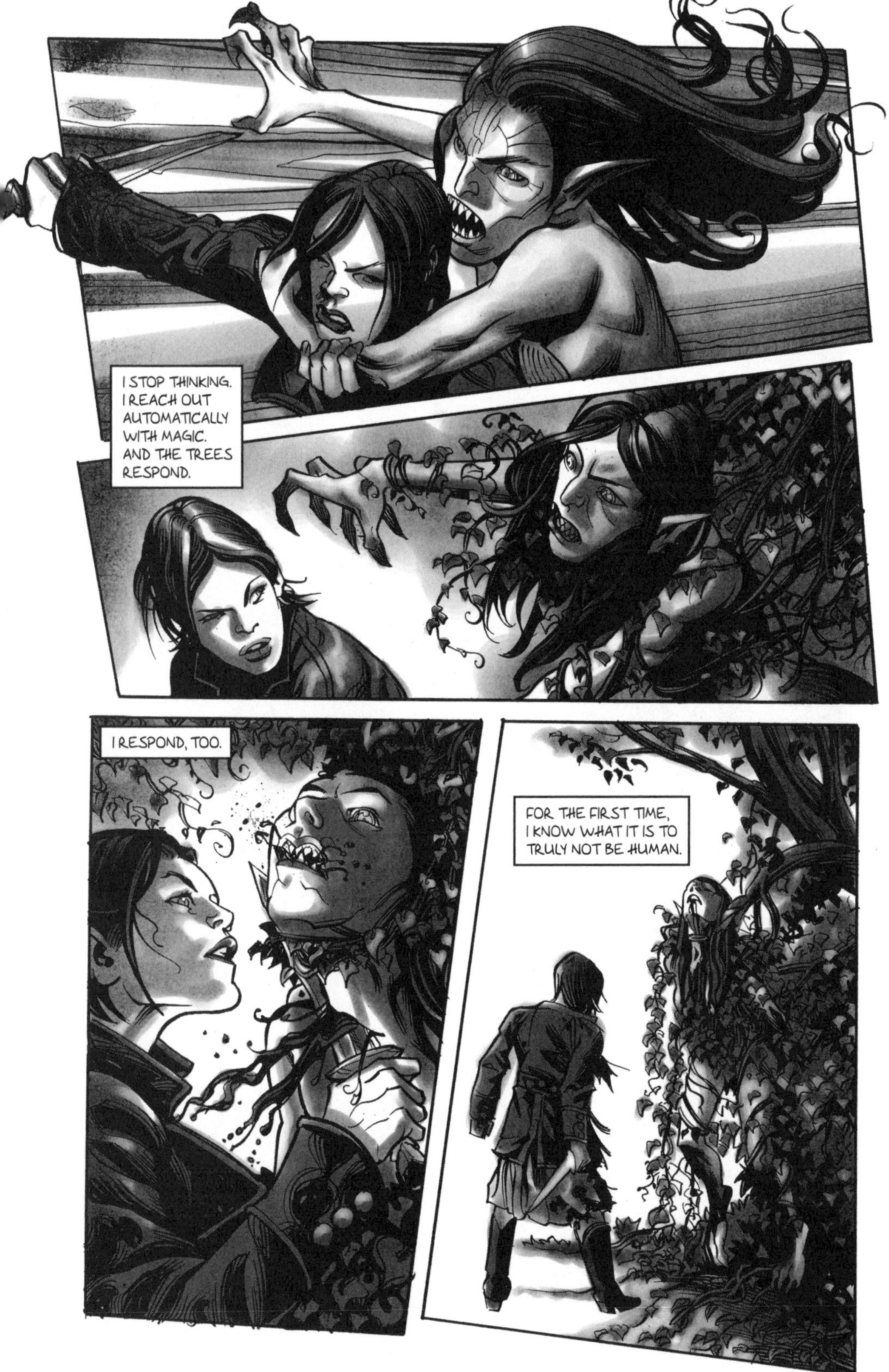
I STOP THINKING.
I REACH OUT
AUTOMATICALLY
WITH MAGIC.
AND THE TREES
RESPOND.
I RESPOND, TOO.
FOR THE FIRST TIME,
I KNOW WHAT IT IS TO
TRULY NOT BE HUMAN.

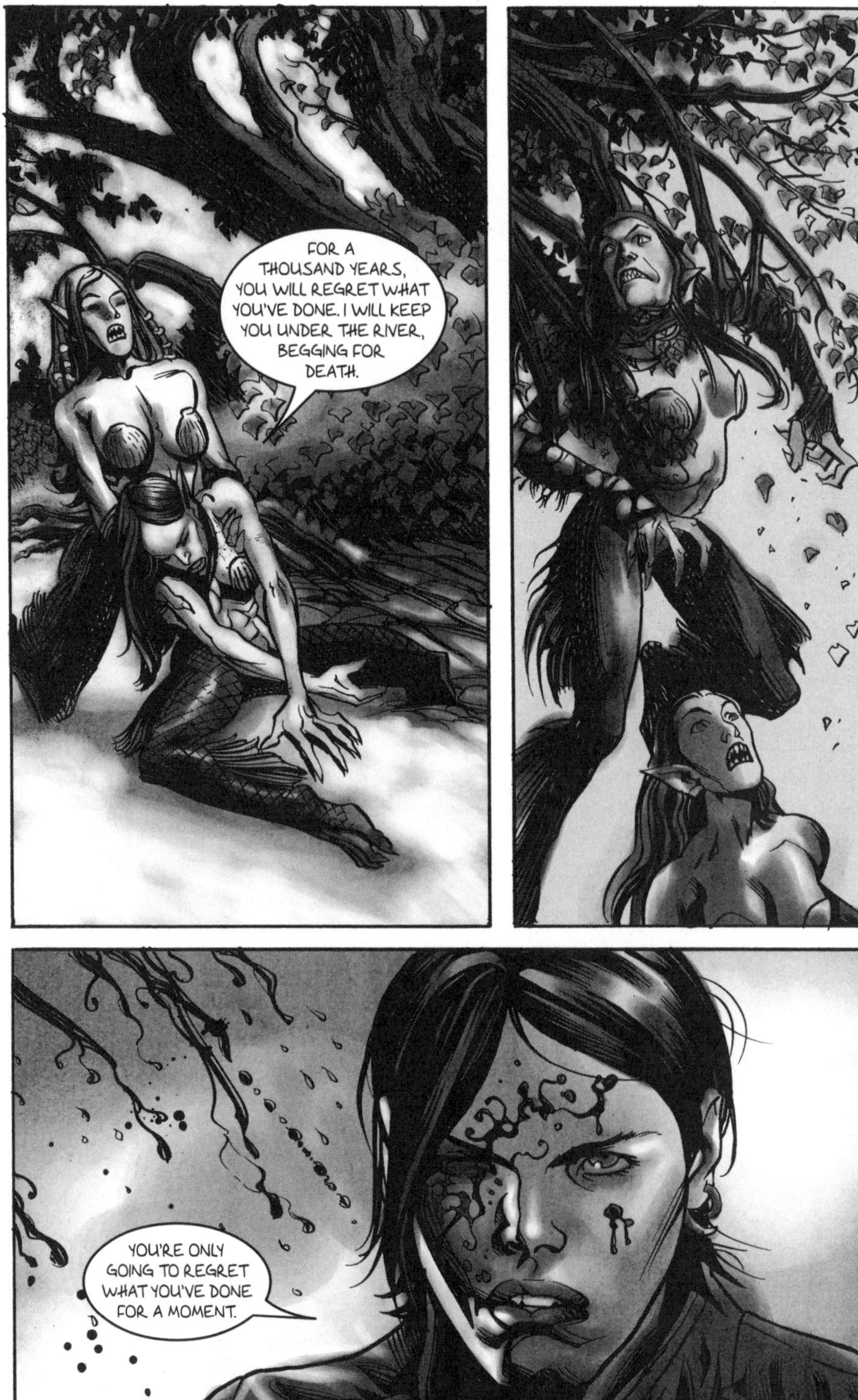
FOR A THOUSAND YEARS, YOU WILL REGRET WHAT YOU'VE DONE. I WILL KEEP YOU UNDER THE RIVER, BEGGING FOR DEATH.
YOU'RE ONLY GOING TO REGRET WHAT YOU'VE DONE FOR A MOMENT.

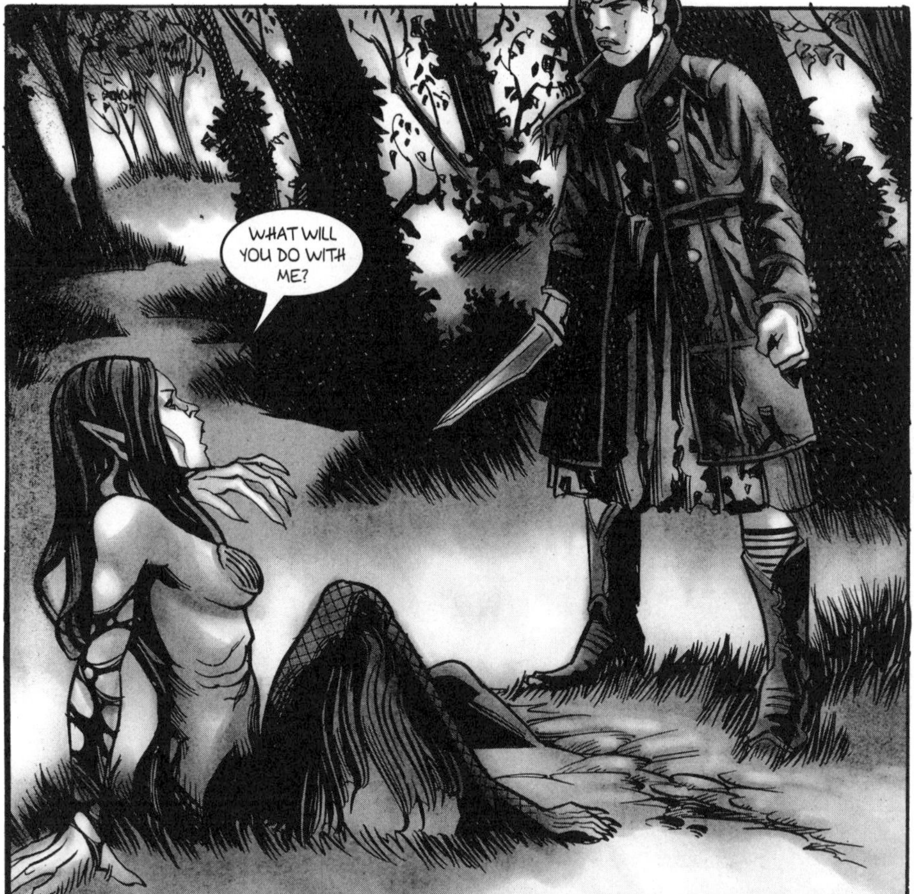
WHAT WILL YOU DO WITH ME?

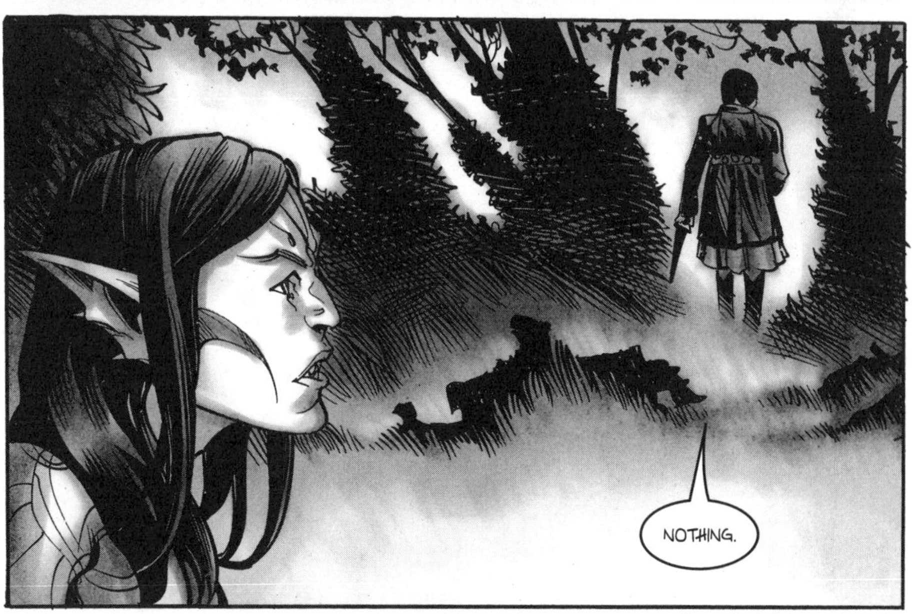
NOTHING.

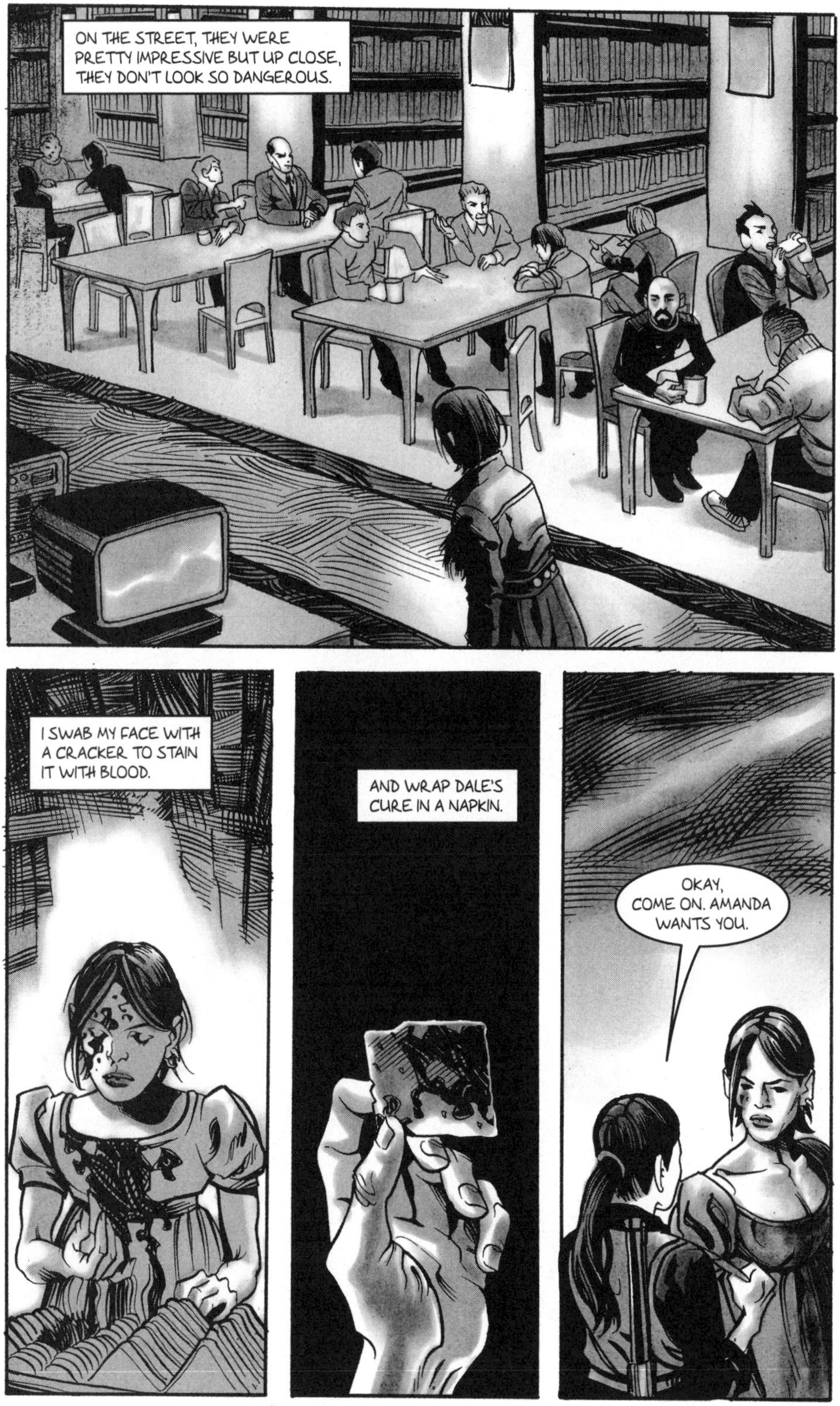
ON THE STREET, THEY WERE PRETTY IMPRESSIVE BUT UP CLOSE, THEY DON'T LOOK SO DANGEROUS.
I SWAB MY FACE WITH A CRACKER TO STAIN IT WITH BLOOD.
AND WRAP DALE'S CURE IN A NAPKIN.
OKAY, COME ON. AMANDA WANTS YOU.

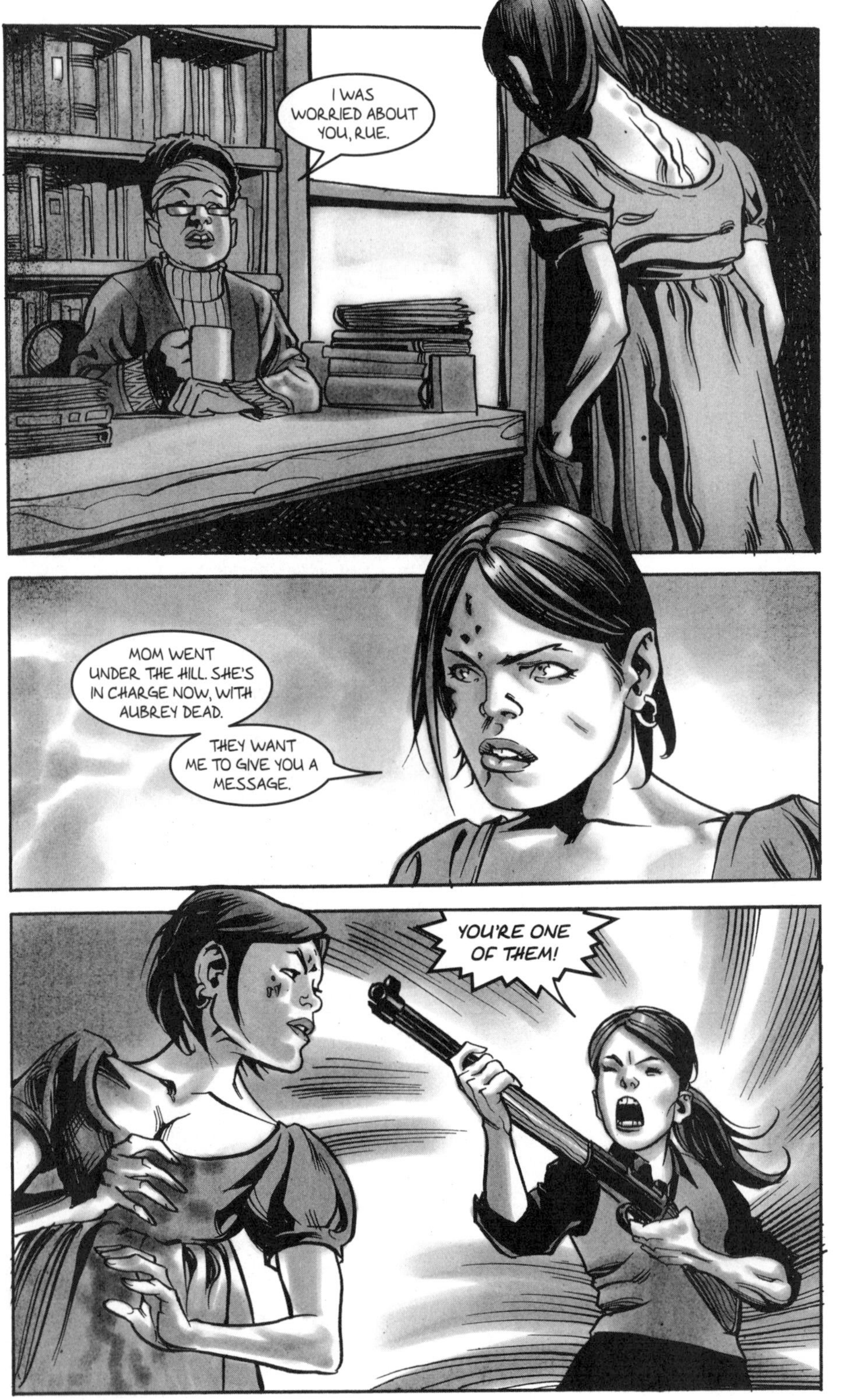
I WAS WORRIED ABOUT YOU, RUE.
MOM WENT UNDER THE HILL. SHE'S IN CHARGE NOW, WITH AUBREY DEAD.
THEY WANT ME TO GIVE YOU A MESSAGE.
YOU'RE ONE OF THEM!

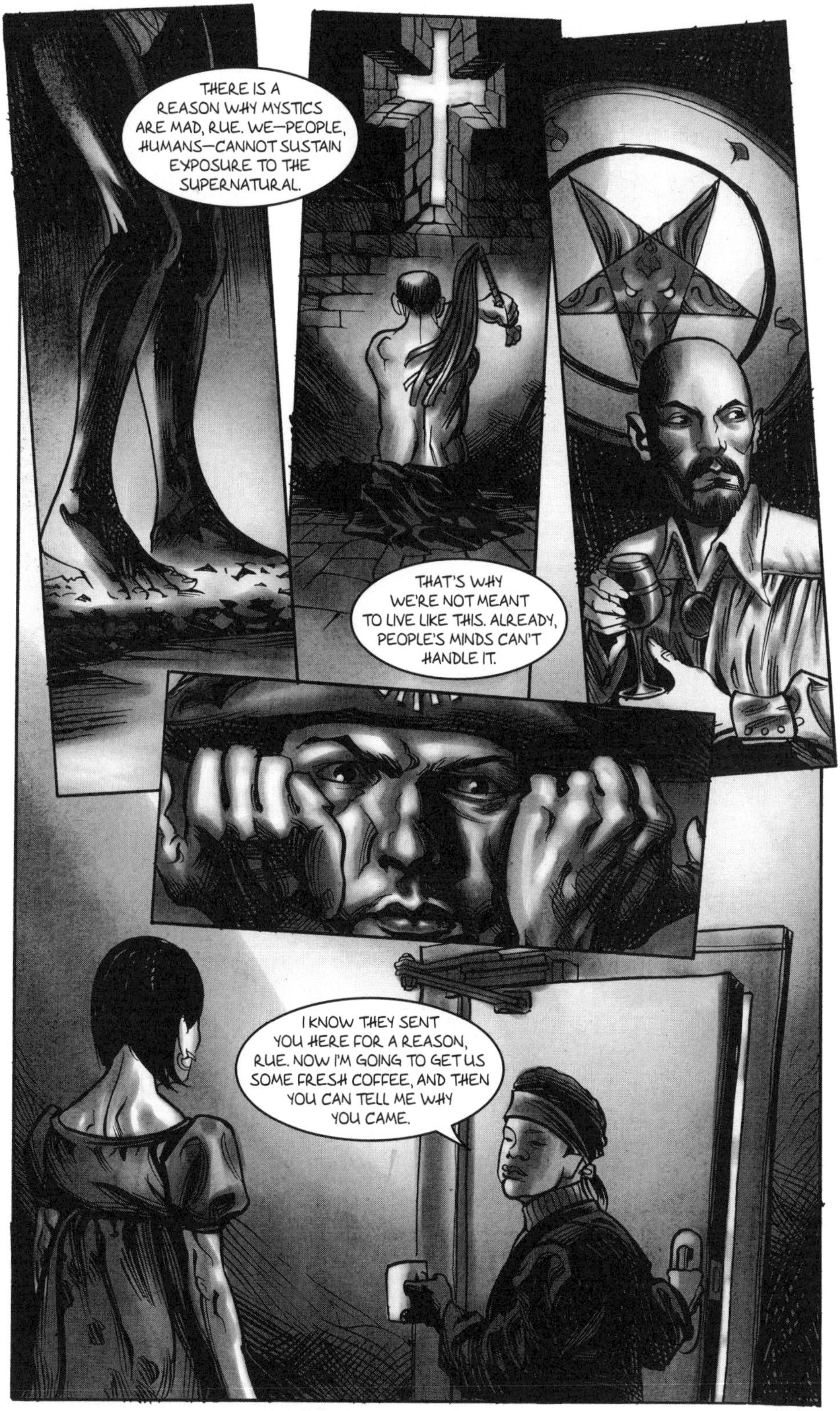
THERE IS A REASON WHY MYSTICS ARE MAD, RUE. WE—PEOPLE, HUMANS—CANNOT SUSTAIN EXPOSURE TO THE SUPERNATURAL.
THAT'S WHY WE'RE NOT MEANT TO LIVE LIKE THIS. ALREADY, PEOPLE'S MINDS CAN'T HANDLE IT.
I KNOW THEY SENT YOU HERE FOR A REASON, RUE. NOW I'M GOING TO GET US SOME FRESH COFFEE, AND THEN YOU CAN TELL ME WHY YOU CAME.

51

65

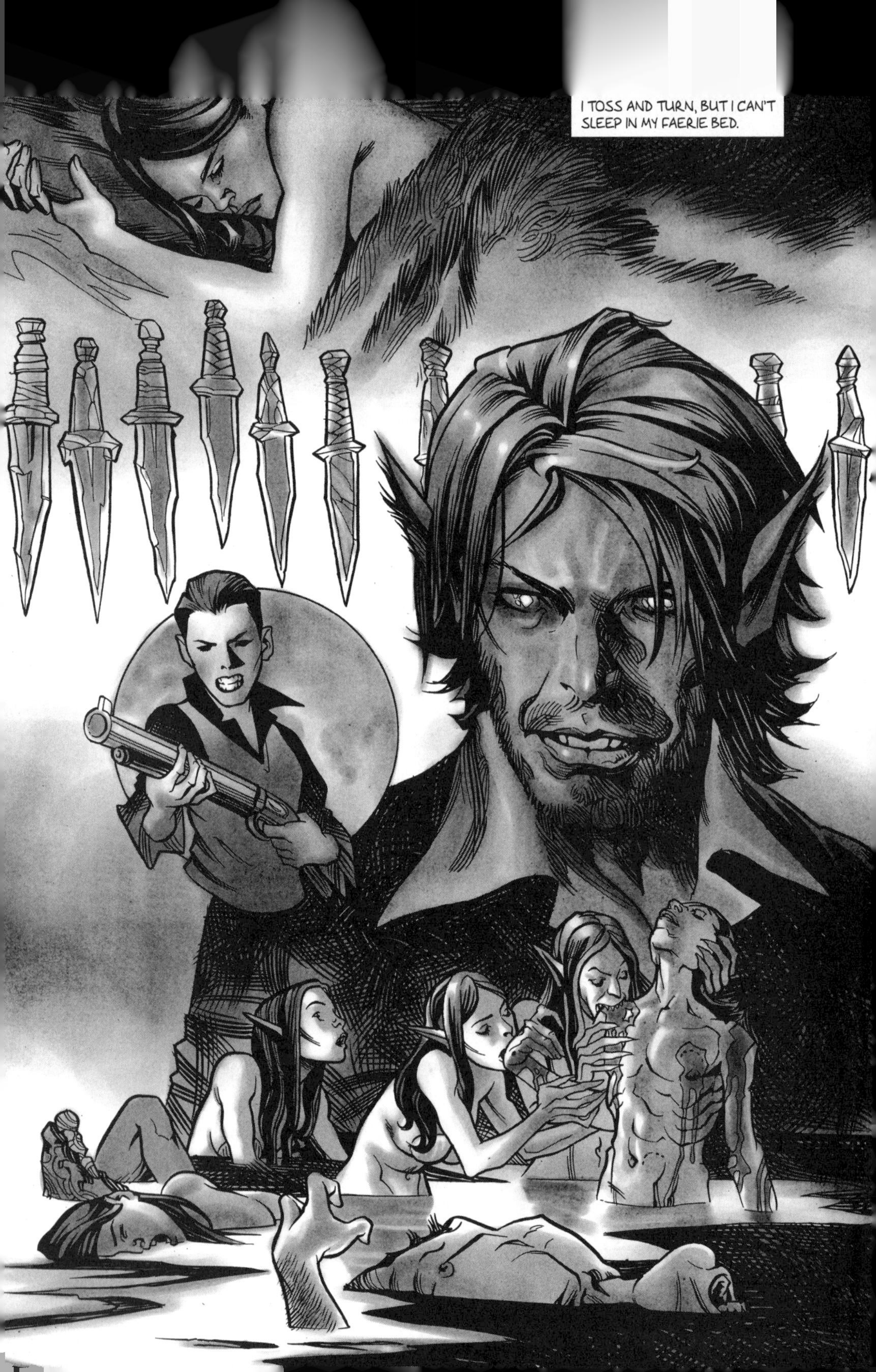
I TOSS AND TURN, BUT I CAN'T SLEEP IN MY FAERIE BED.

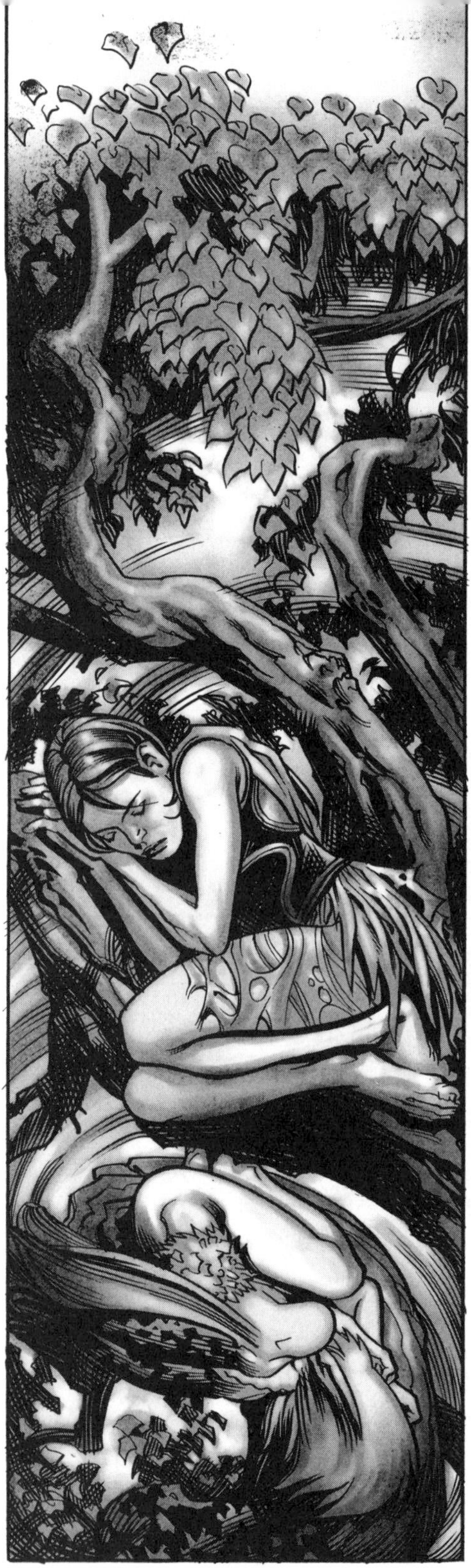

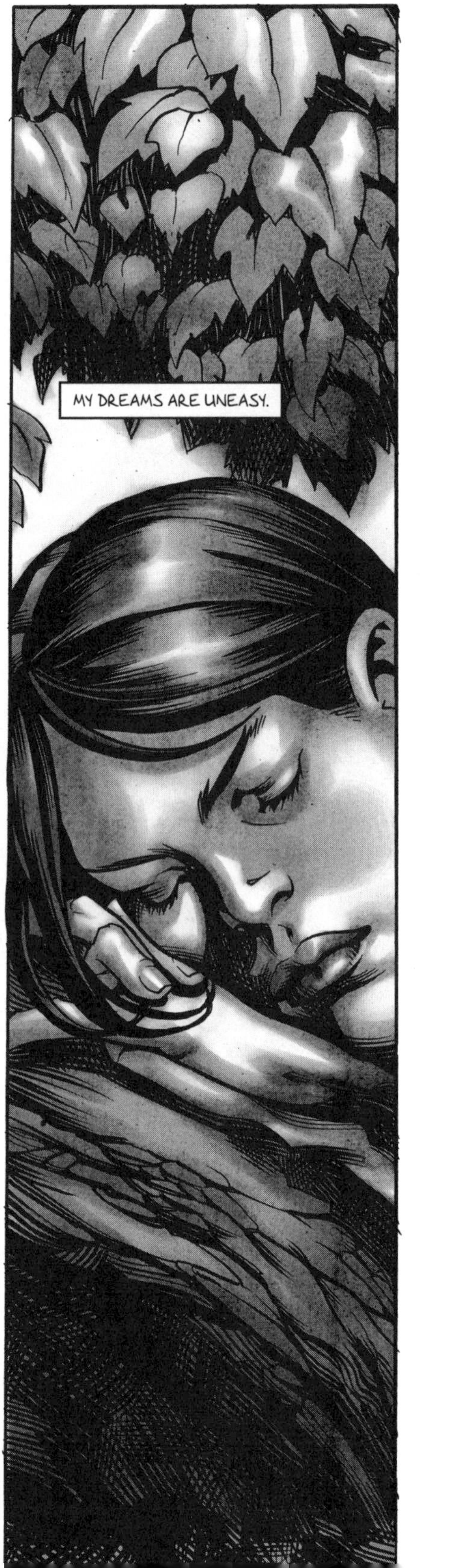
MY DREAMS ARE UNEASY.

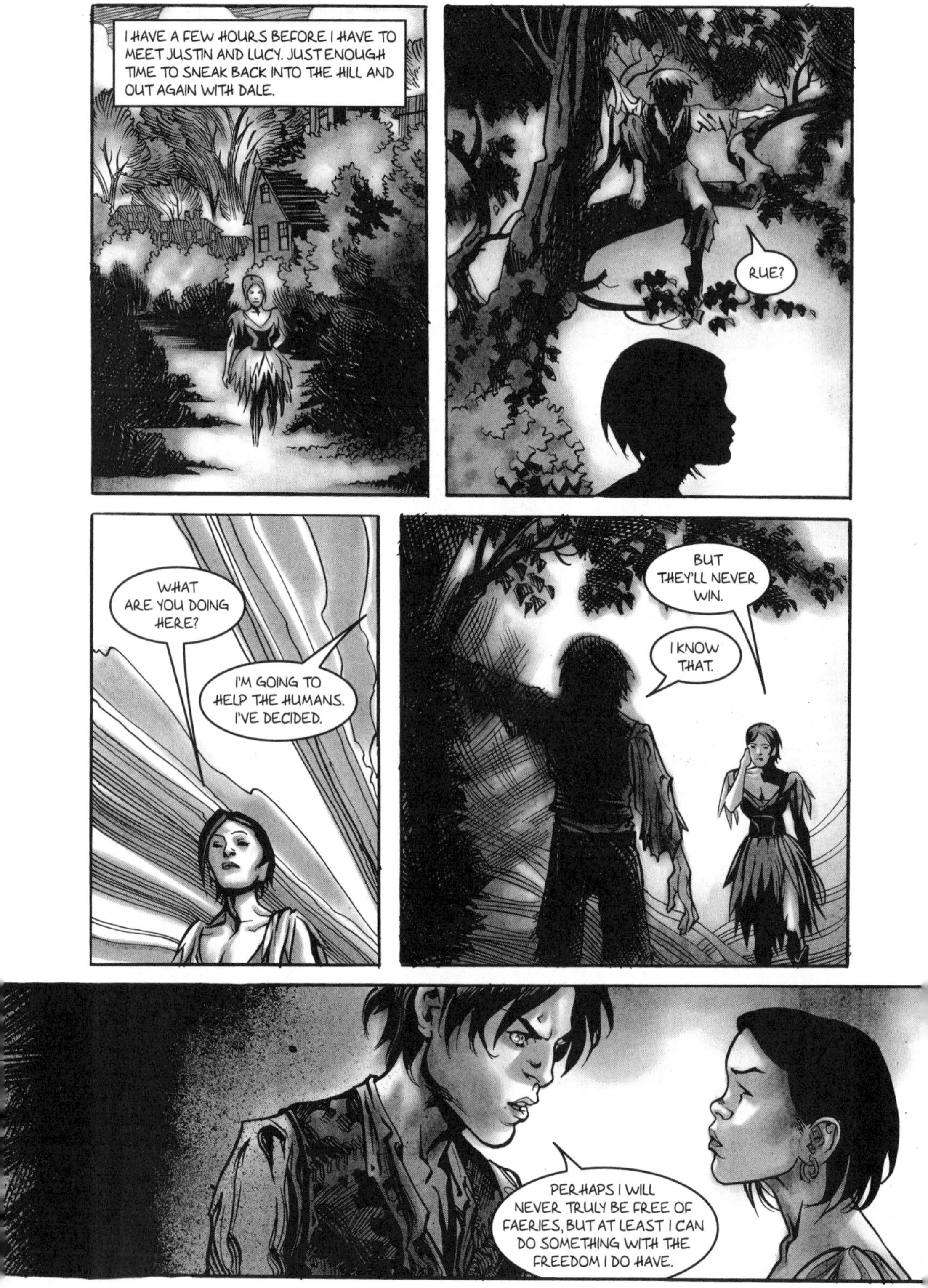
I HAVE A FEW HOURS BEFORE I HAVE TO MEET JUSTIN AND LUCY. JUST ENOUGH TIME TO SNEAK BACK INTO THE HILL AND OUT AGAIN WITH DALE.
RUE?
WHAT ARE YOU DOING HERE?
I'M GOING TO HELP THE HUMANS. I'VE DECIDED.
BUT THEY'LL NEVER WIN.
I KNOW THAT.
PERHAPS I WILL NEVER TRULY BE FREE OF FAERIES, BUT AT LEAST I CAN DO SOMETHING WITH THE FREEDOM I DO HAVE.

72

73

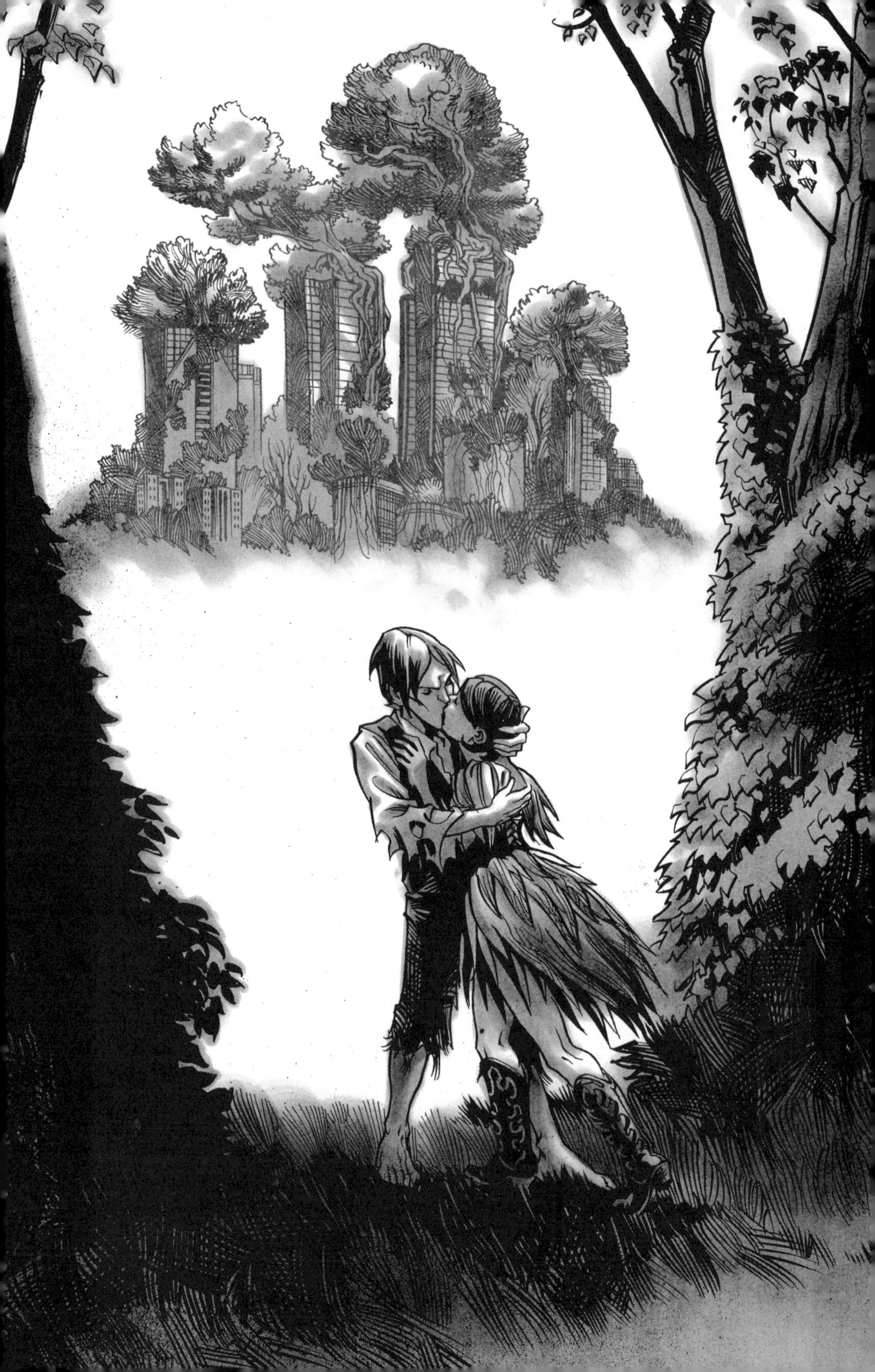

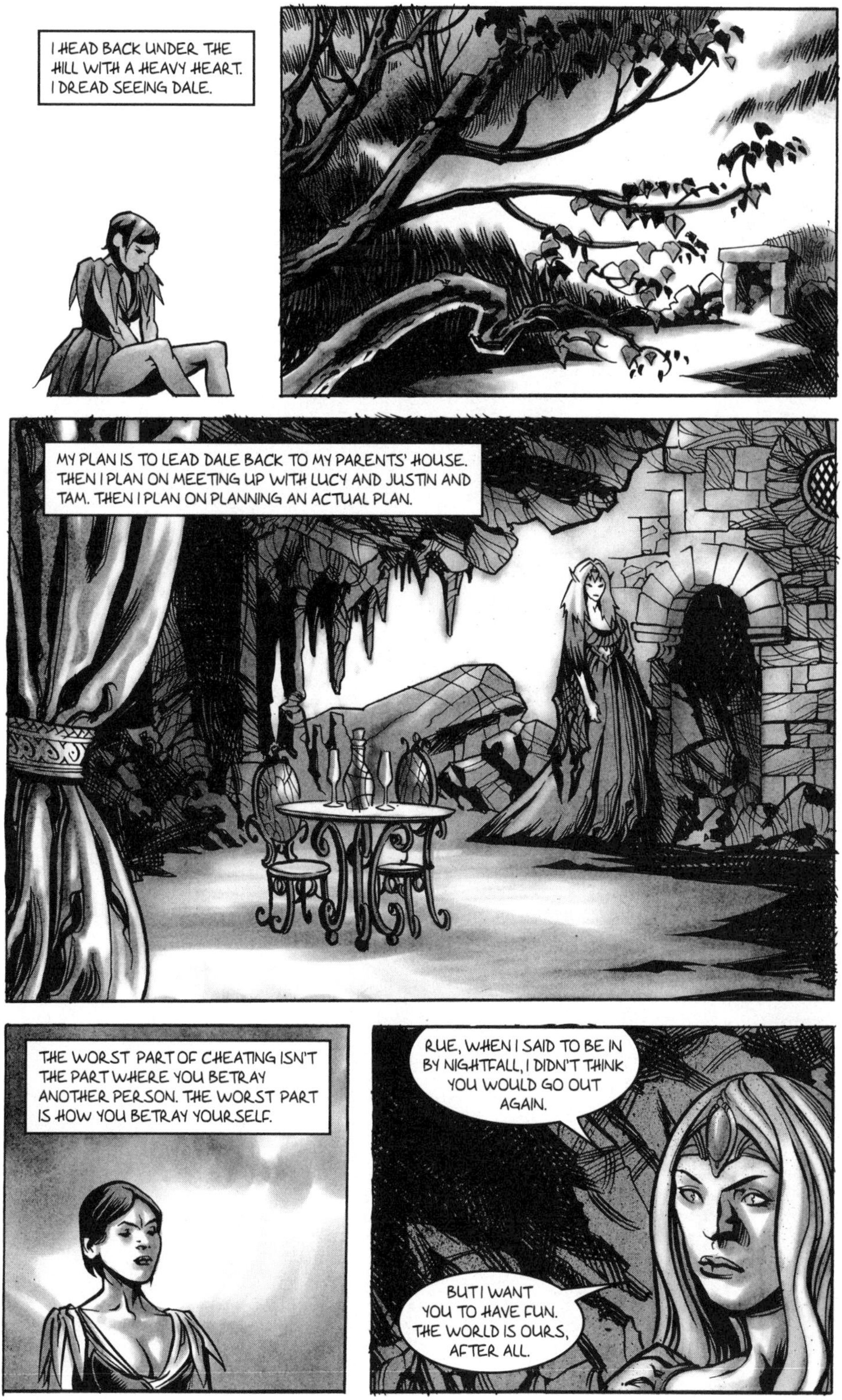
I HEAD BACK UNDER THE HILL WITH A HEAVY HEART. I DREAD SEEING DALE.
MY PLAN IS TO LEAD DALE BACK TO MY PARENTS' HOUSE. THEN I PLAN ON MEETING UP WITH LUCY AND JUSTIN AND TAM. THEN I PLAN ON PLANNING AN ACTUAL PLAN.
THE WORST PART OF CHEATING ISN'T THE PART WHERE YOU BETRAY ANOTHER PERSON. THE WORST PART IS HOW YOU BETRAY YOURSELF.
RUE, WHEN I SAID TO BE IN BY NIGHTFALL, I DIDN'T THINK YOU WOULD GO OUT AGAIN.
BUT I WANT YOU TO HAVE FUN. THE WORLD IS OURS, AFTER ALL.

79

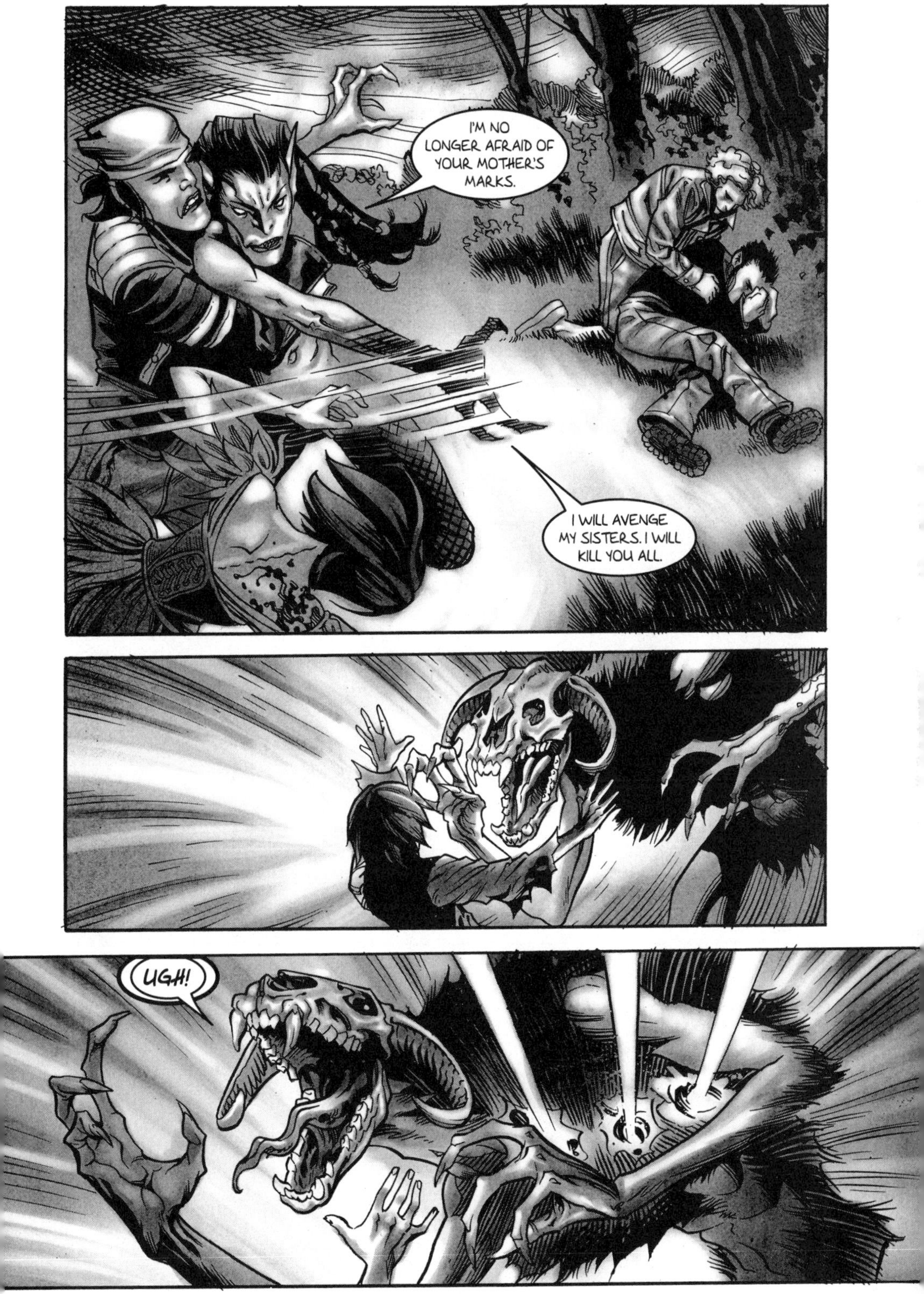
I'M NO LONGER AFRAID OF YOUR MOTHER'S MARKS.
I WILL AVENGE MY SISTERS. I WILL KILL YOU ALL.
UGH!

85

88

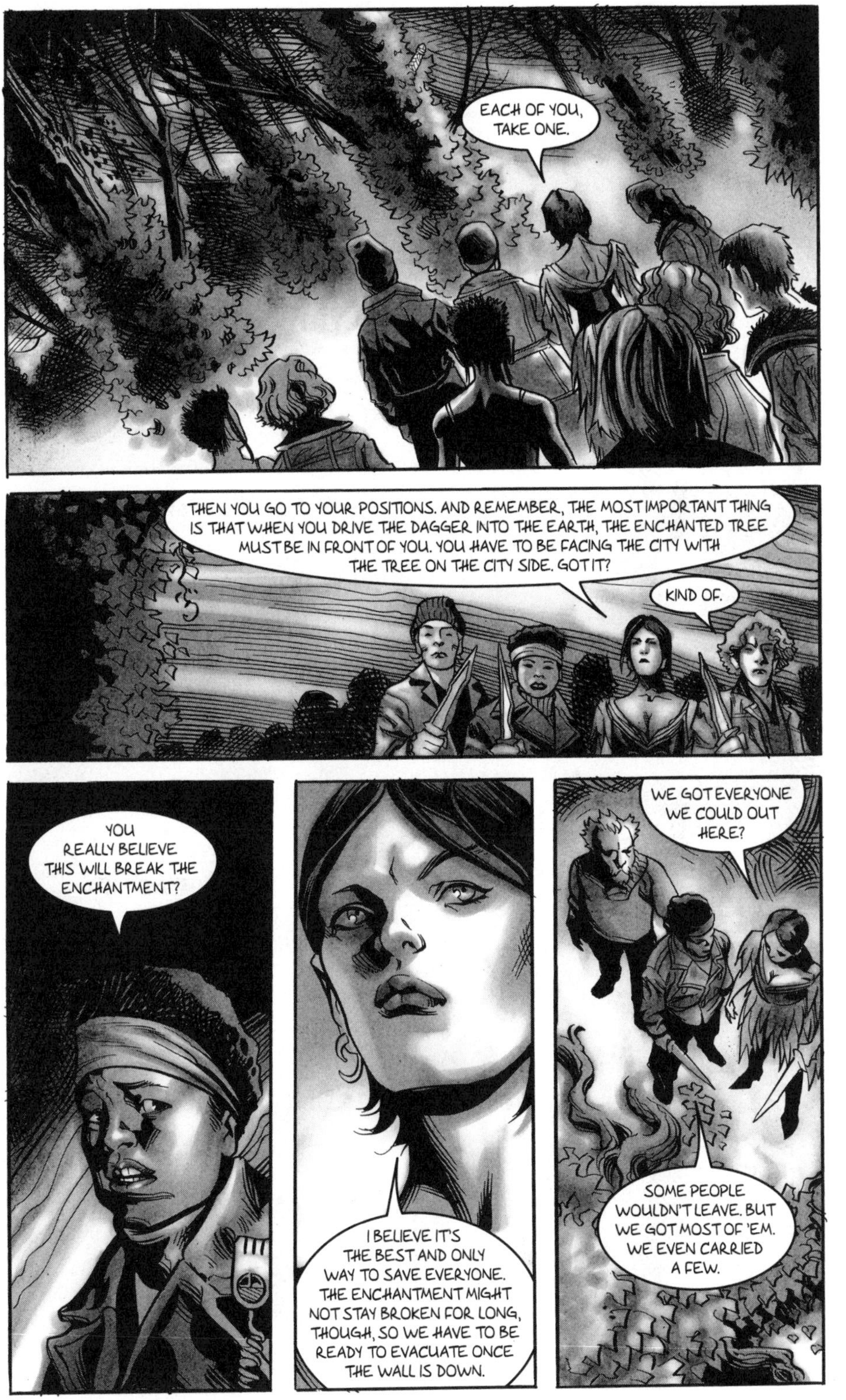
EACH OF YOU, TAKE ONE.
THEN YOU GO TO YOUR POSITIONS. AND REMEMBER, THE MOST IMPORTANT THING IS THAT WHEN YOU DRIVE THE DAGGER INTO THE EARTH, THE ENCHANTED TREE MUST BE IN FRONT OF YOU. YOU HAVE TO BE FACING THE CITY WITH THE TREE ON THE CITY SIDE. GOT IT?
KIND OF.
YOU REALLY BELIEVE THIS WILL BREAK THE ENCHANTMENT?
I BELIEVE IT'S THE BEST AND ONLY WAY TO SAVE EVERYONE. THE ENCHANTMENT MIGHT NOT STAY BROKEN FOR LONG, THOUGH, SO WE HAVE TO BE READY TO EVACUATE ONCE THE WALL IS DOWN.
WE GOT EVERYONE WE COULD OUT HERE?
SOME PEOPLE WOULDN'T LEAVE. BUT WE GOT MOST OF 'EM. WE EVEN CARRIED A FEW.

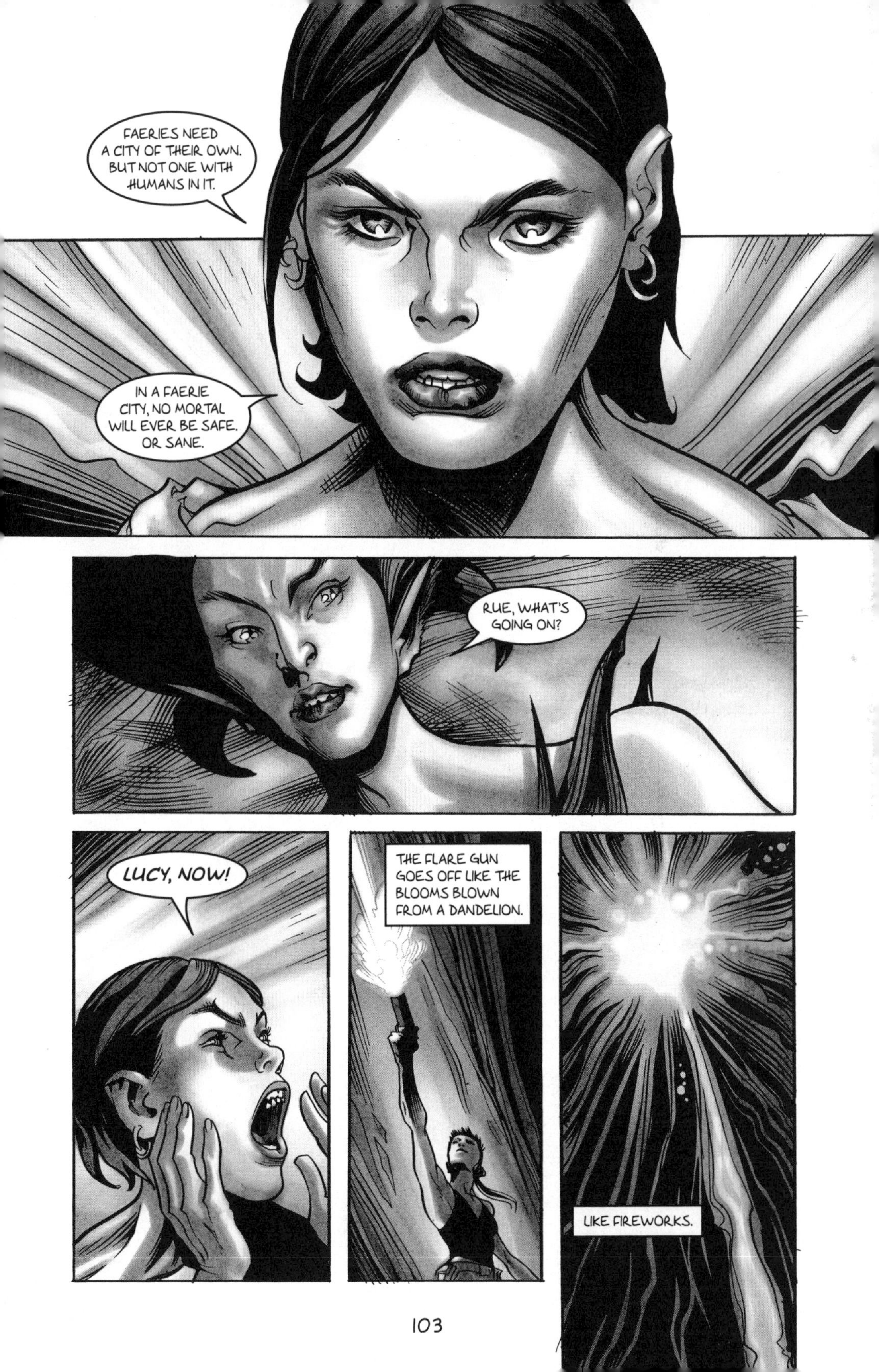
FAERIES NEED A CITY OF THEIR OWN. BUT NOT ONE WITH HUMANS IN IT.
IN A FAERIE CITY, NO MORTAL WILL EVER BE SAFE. OR SANE.
RUE, WHAT'S GOING ON?
LUCY, NOW!
THE FLARE GUN GOES OFF LIKE THE BLOOMS BLOWN FROM A DANDELION.
LIKE FIREWORKS.

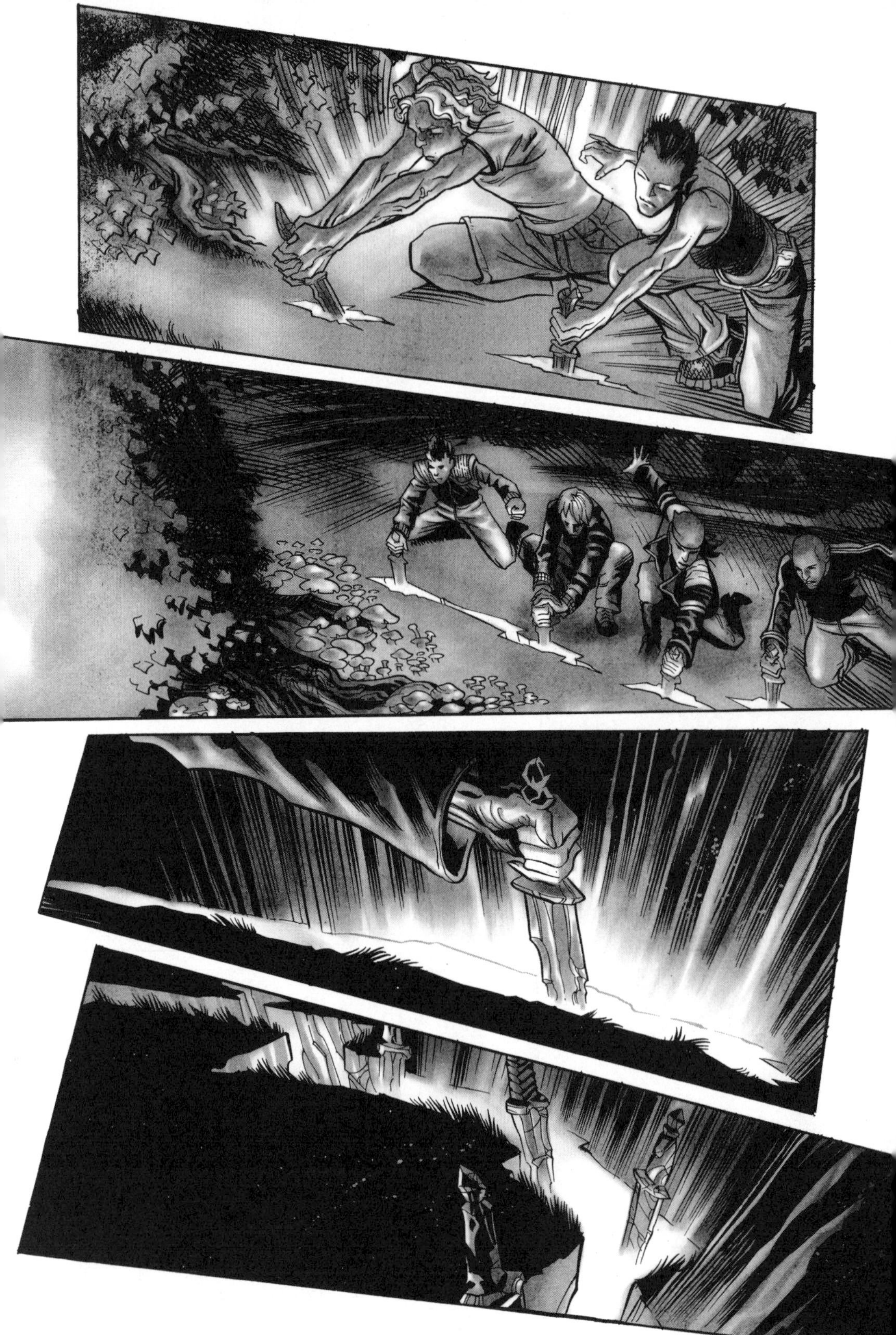

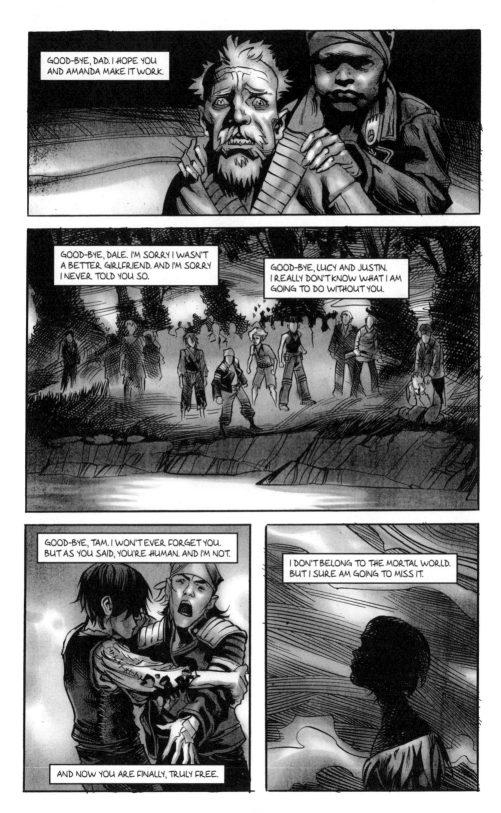

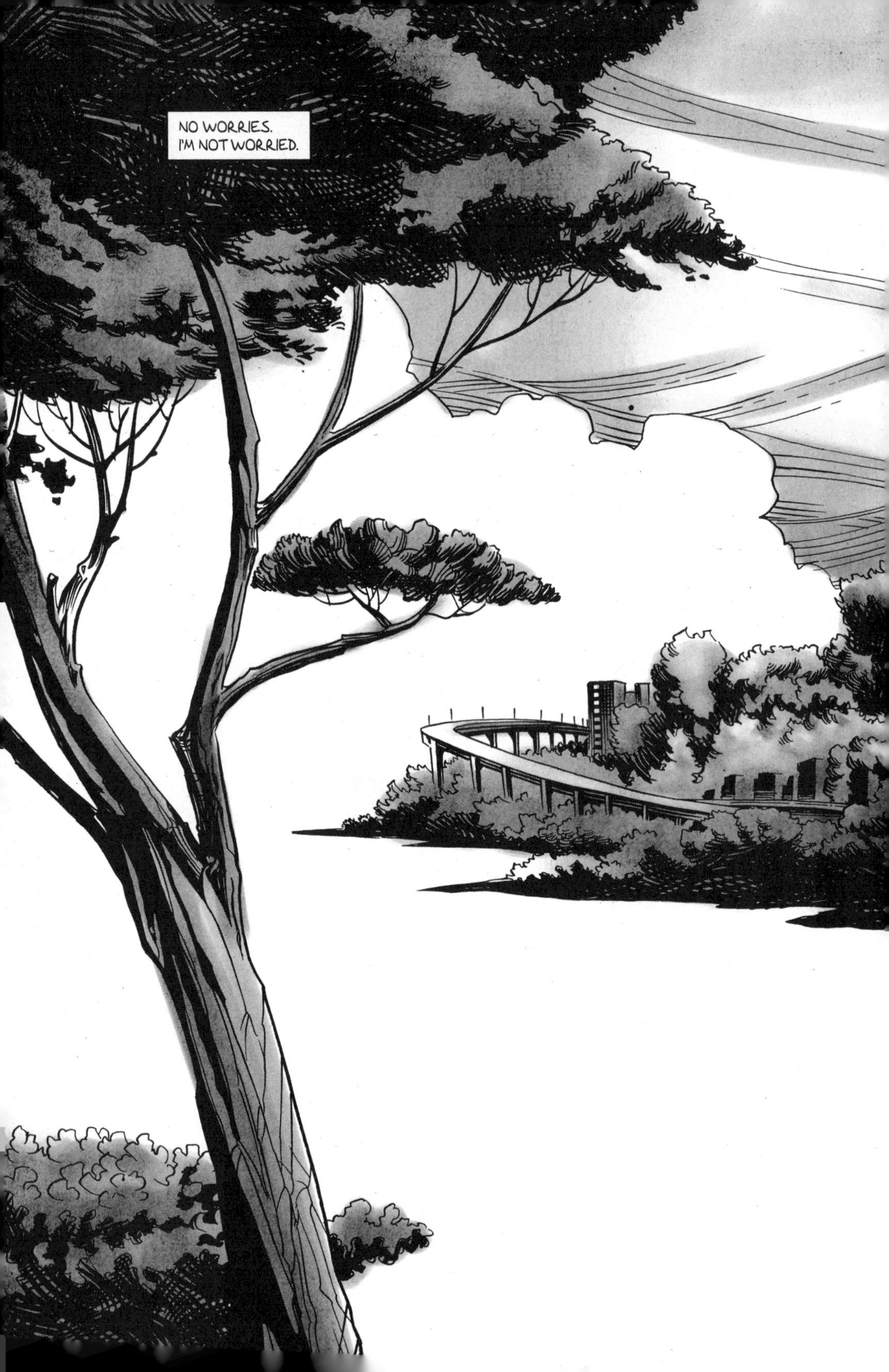
NO WORRIES.
I'M NOT WORRIED.

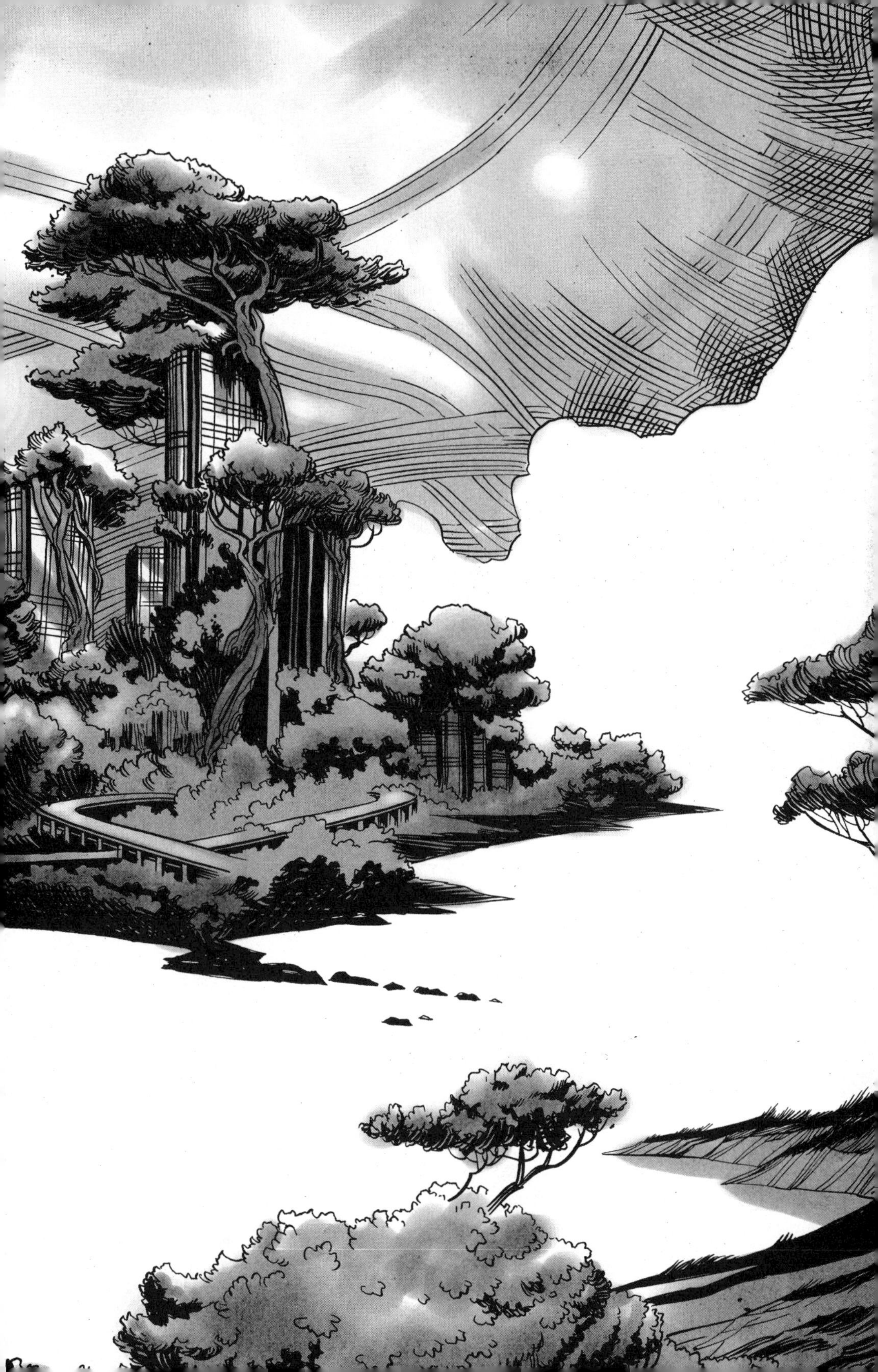

end

ABOUT THE AUTHOR

Holly Black is the author of contemporary fantasy novels for teens and children. Born in New Jersey, Holly grew up in a decrepit Victorian house piled with books and oddments. She never quite recovered.

Her first book, *Tithe: A Modern Faerie Tale*, was called "dark, edgy, beautifully written and compulsively readable" by *Booklist*, received starred reviews from *Publisher's Weekly* and *Kirkus*, and was included in the American Library Association's Best Books for Young Adults. Holly has since written two other books in the same universe: *Valiant*, a recipient of the Andre Norton Award for Excellence in Young Adult Literature, and *Ironside*.

Holly collaborated with her long-time friend, Caldecott Honor–winning artist Tony DiTerlizzi, to create the best-selling Spiderwick Chronicles. The serial has been called "vintage Victorian fantasy" by the *New York Post*, and *Time* reported that "the books wallow in their dusty Olde Worlde charm." The Spiderwick Chronicles were adapted into a film in 2008.

Holly's latest novel is a curse magic caper called *The White Cat*, the first in the Curse Workers series.

She lives in Massachusetts with her husband, Theo, and an ever-expanding collection of books. She spends a lot of her time in cafes, glaring at her laptop and drinking endless cups of coffee.